Hearts, Fingers, AND OTHER THINGS to Cross

Hearts, Fingers, AND OTHER THINGS to Cross

KATIE FINN

SQUARE
FISH

Feiwel and Friends
New York

SQUARE
FISH

An imprint of Macmillan Publishing Group, LLC
175 Fifth Avenue
New York, NY 10010
fiercereads.com

Our books may be purchased in bulk for promotional, educational,
or business use. Please contact your local bookseller or the Macmillan
Corporate and Premium Sales Department at (800) 221-7945 ext. 5442
or by e-mail at MacmillanSpecialMarkets@macmillan.com.

Library of Congress Cataloging-in-Publication Data Available

ISBN 978-1-250-12182-0 (paperback)   ISBN 978-1-250-08687-7 (ebook)

Originally published in the United States by Feiwel and Friends
First Square Fish Edition: 2017
Square Fish logo designed by Filomena Tuosto

1   3   5   7   9   10   8   6   4   2

For Jessi Kirby and Jessica Brody.
Excellent writers, wonderful friends.

Gemma Rose Tucker

Hallie's Birthday Party—THE PLAN

—Sneak onto the party boat without getting caught
 (pretend to be caterer. Do hair and makeup first!).
—Pack fancy dress (borrow from one of Bruce's
 exes. She won't know).
—Make sure Gwyneth finishes putting together the
 Hallie footage.
—~~Talk to Josh about what's going to happen~~
—~~Ask Josh what was up with that moment in the~~
 ~~ice-cream freezer.~~
—~~Tell Josh you're not sure what you're feeling about~~
 ~~him because lately you've been having feelings for~~
 ~~Ford~~
—Avoid Josh.
—Avoid Teddy.
—If Teddy approaches, go in the other direction.
 (But what was up with that kiss the other day?
 He's HALLIE'S boyfriend now. You know, since he
 dumped me out of the blue in Target and I later
 found out he'd been cheating on me with her for
 months. BUT they're together now, and he

shouldn't be kissing me, even if it was just a
cheek-kiss-gone-wrong. Do I need to remind him
about that?)

—No. <u>Just avoid Teddy!</u>

—Talk to Sophie about Reid. If she really just wants
to be friends with him, maybe she should pick a
different dress to wear? The poor guy's only
human, after all. And it's TOTALLY obvious he's in
love with her.

—Talk to Sophie about maybe not dating only bad
boys. Especially since they always turn out, well,
bad.

—Remember to call Dad in California after the party.
He's probably still mad—not surprising, after Hallie
sent him my old journal—the one that detailed all
the things I was trying to do to make her
miserable when we were eleven. But Dad needs to
understand that things might have been different
if he'd TOLD me about the fact that he was
dating Hallie's mother, Karen. Instead I found
out by accident, and was terrified it meant he
and my mother would never get back together. So
of course I panicked and tried to make Hallie
miserable so Karen would take her away. And
then things got really out of control, and Karen's
career got wrecked. But the journal doesn't show
that Hallie spent the last five years plotting her

revenge on ME—stealing Teddy and spending the whole summer getting back at me.

-(If necessary, remind Dad that Karen now has a hugely successful career as a pseudonymous author of vampire erotica. So, really, things worked out for the best.)

-Tell Dad that Hallie tried to get me framed for a crime and ARRESTED earlier this summer, in addition to charging nine hundred dollars' worth of cheese onto his credit card (don't need to mention that I tricked Hallie into getting her hair cut short or that I got her fired from her babysitting job. These are the kinds of small details he doesn't really need to know).

-Blend in at the party—be there when the video plays that shows JUST how horrible Hallie is. How many terrible things she did to me over the course of the summer. How she tricked Teddy into being with her in the first place and stole him away from me. Teddy and everyone will finally see the truth about her!

-Try to grab a mini-cupcake for Ford. He loves those.

-charge phone.

-Buy more stationery.

CHAPTER 1

I shifted in my hard straight-backed chair and tried to ignore the fact that I could feel frosting starting to dry on my cheek. I had been uncomfortable many times in my life—and certainly *many* times this summer, like when I'd been at a pool party and my bathing suit had started to disintegrate—but this probably took the cake. Sitting in the world's least comfortable chair, wearing a borrowed dress that had gotten ripped at the shoulder, frosting in my hair, and getting yelled at by an angry ship's captain for fighting while my dad shook his head disapprovingly . . . it won My Most Uncomfortable Moment, hands down.

"I've just never experienced anything like this before!" the captain was saying as he tried to pace around his office. It seemed like maybe he was used to pacing when he was upset, but this was made more difficult by the fact that the office wasn't very big to start with, and now it was filled with me, my dad, Hallie Bridges, and her mom, Karen—not to mention all the baggage we'd dragged in there with us. "I mean, the last thing I expect when agreeing to have a birthday party on my boat is that the guests will end up brawling and throwing cake at each other, to the point where they have to be physically separated!"

I glanced over at Hallie, who was in the chair next to me. She was sitting up ramrod straight, and I could see that it looked like the heel of one of her shoes was broken off, and her short pixie cut was beyond mussed—and slightly blue, due to the frosting I'd rubbed into it when we were fighting. I closed my eyes for just a second, still not quite able to believe it had happened. It was something I *never* normally would have done . . . but then again, this whole summer could fit under that heading. I hadn't planned to fight with Hallie tonight. Sure, I'd gone to the party with the goal of playing the video compilation that showed the worst of Hallie. It was straight from the source, too, Hallie revealing the truth about who she was—but accidentally, because she didn't know I'd spent the last month with a camera clipped to my shirt.

But even though I'd intended to show the video to everyone—and, once and for all, put an end to this revenge war of ours—I'd had a change of heart at the last minute and called it off. I'd been ready to walk away from all of it. But the video had gotten played anyway, thanks to Gwyneth Davidson and her own secret agenda, which had been unknown to me until the moment it was too late to stop it. Hallie had stalked over to me, furious, as soon as it was over, and while I'd started to explain it hadn't been me, she hadn't given me the chance to continue. She'd shoved me, hard, and when I pushed back to steady myself, something in me had snapped. All the buildup of a summer of secrets and lies and escalating revenge plans had suddenly come rushing out, and the next thing I knew, Hallie and I had been fighting—dress-ripping, cake-throwing *fighting* in front of everyone, in front of the whole party.

"Do you have anything to say for yourselves?" the captain asked now, looking from me to Hallie.

Hallie turned and looked at me, and I could see there was still fury in her eyes. "I have something to say about the security on this boat," she snapped. She pointed at me, even though it wasn't really necessary in a room this small. "Somehow this *person* was able to board the boat and then ruin my party, when she was explicitly not invited."

"Oh, you think *I* ruined your party?" I asked, turning to face her. "I think you did that on your own."

"Listen," Hallie snapped, her voice low and seething. "If you think—"

"Girls!" This was my dad, looking back and forth between us, bewildered. "Really. This is getting out of control."

I opened my mouth to respond, but then all words left me as once again my gaze drifted down to Karen's hand—to her *left* hand, and to the giant ring currently sitting there.

The sight of it had been enough to knock all words from me as Hallie and I were pulled apart by our respective parents. Just seeing my dad there had been a major shock on its own—he had told me he was in California, where he lived during the year, working on his latest screenplay. So to see him, in the Hamptons, on the boat for Hallie's seventeenth-birthday party, had thrown me for a loop. But I wasn't done being shocked just yet—Hallie had noticed the ring on her mother's hand at the same moment I had. Before we could get an explanation, though, we'd been hustled in here by the captain while the DJ had started playing music again, clearly trying to get the party going after Hallie and I had so decidedly derailed it.

And now, as I looked from my dad to Karen, I couldn't quite believe it was happening, even as the evidence was right in front of me. They had gotten engaged—*engaged*—without even talking to me about it first? My dad hadn't even told me he was dating Karen again, which I thought he might have been able to mention, if he was serious enough about her to propose. Looking back, I should have read the signs—my dad had been happy and distracted, in a fuzzy state for the last month. And he had stopped complaining about having to adapt the film version of *Just Bitten*, the best-selling erotic vampire trilogy. When I'd figured out that the author was actually Karen writing under a pseudonym, I should have put two and two together, especially considering all the time my dad had been spending with the author. But I'd been so caught up in my own drama, I'd missed what was right in front of my face.

"You want to talk about out of control?" Hallie asked now, turning to face her mother. She pointed at Karen's hand, and I realized Hallie had just been thinking the same thing I was. After a summer of either never knowing what she was thinking—or being two steps behind her—it was a bit of a shock. "What's going on there? Don't you think you might have *mentioned* it?"

"Yeah," I said immediately. Hallie turned to look at me, and it seemed like she was as surprised as I was that we were on the same side of things for once.

"That's not the issue here," Karen said as she folded her hands behind her back, her cheeks going pink.

"Exactly," the captain said, starting to look increasingly uncomfortable that we were bringing personal business into this. "The issue at hand is the behavior that was exhibited, not to mention the damage done, not only to this vessel, but to its reputation. We can't be seen as an operation where fights break out and destruction is allowed to flourish."

"I wouldn't have felt the need for destruction," Hallie snapped, "if someone hadn't snuck onto the boat *illegally* and humiliated me in front of all my guests!" Her voice cracked on the last word, and she scowled, like she was angry at herself for showing even the tiniest flicker of emotion. She sat up straighter and crossed her arms over her chest—then uncrossed them when she looked down and must have realized the front of her dress was covered in cake.

"And like I've been trying to tell you," I said, feeling the need to defend myself, especially given the way my dad was currently looking at me, "*it wasn't me.* I tried to call it off, but Gwyneth went ahead and played it."

"Gwyneth . . . Bruce's daughter?" my dad interjected, looking not angry any longer, just baffled. "Why would she do that?" He looked around, like she might be hiding somewhere in the office. "Is she here?"

"She's at the party," I said, trying to keep my voice steady but not able to stop myself from seeing Gwyneth and Josh on the side of the boat, kissing. I wasn't even sure what I was feeling for Josh . . . and I was pretty sure I had moved on from him after he'd made it abundantly clear he was done with me. But still, seeing him and Gwyneth kissing—and seeing the way he'd looked at her—had hit me harder than I'd been prepared for it to.

"Wait, the Gwyneth who's dating Josh?" Karen asked, now sounding as puzzled as my dad.

"No, a *different* Gwyneth," Hallie snapped. Karen's eyebrows flew up, and a moment later I saw Hallie pale slightly, like she'd just realized she'd crossed a line. "Sorry," she muttered.

"Why would Gwyneth have done that?" my dad asked.

"Exactly," Hallie said, turning to glare at me again. "It makes no sense. Gemma's clearly making it up."

"It's because she's making a *documentary*," I said, glaring right back at her. "About us. And she needed your reaction for the third act, or something."

"I thought her documentary was about Bruce," my dad said, his brow furrowed. I wasn't sure how to tell him I didn't think it was going to get unfurrowed in the near future. "And me," he added after a moment, no doubt thinking back to the last month we'd all spent staying in Bruce's house, tiny cameras clipped onto our shirts, giving them back to Gwyneth every night so she could bank the footage.

"She said it was too boring," I said, and it looked like a tiny flicker of hurt crossed my dad's face before he returned to looking bewildered. "Um, sorry."

"Wait, someone was *filming* on the boat today?" the captain asked, and I blinked as I looked over at him. I'd almost forgotten he was there. "I wasn't made aware of that. Did they get the proper permits?"

"You really expect me to believe that?" Hallie asked me, ignoring the captain completely, but with less confidence than before—like some of this was starting to ring true to her.

"Believe what you want," I said. "It's the truth." I looked over at my dad and Karen. "And she was the one who leaked Karen's identity to the press," I said, hoping they would believe me and not just think I was passing the blame on to Gwyneth. "Not me. She said she needed to create more drama."

"So much for a documentary," Hallie muttered, and I tried not to let the shock appear on my face that we had now agreed on two things in the span of a few minutes. I was sure it was an anomaly, that was all.

"Wait just a minute," my dad said, shaking his head. "This doesn't make any sense."

I shook my head. "It does, though," I said. "Gwyneth is a lot more like Bruce than you realize. And what would Bruce have done in this situation?"

I saw a look of understanding pass over my dad's face, and he nodded. Bruce Davidson, his former college roommate-turned major Hollywood producer, was ruthless when it came to getting his movies made, a trait his daughter, I'd realized just a bit too late, had clearly inherited.

"Bruce?" the captain repeated, looking between us.

"Never mind," I said quickly, feeling like there was really no need to involve sea captains in this. If we did, I knew Bruce would suddenly get way too interested, and the next thing you knew, he'd be developing a thriller about a party on a boat gone wrong.

"So can we go?" Hallie asked with all the dignity one can muster when there is frosting in your hair.

"Yes," the captain said, looking relieved we were coming back to the issue at hand. "I mean, no. We need to discuss the next steps. The last thing I want is my boat getting a reputation as the kind of vessel where these types of shenanigans happen."

"I assure you . . ." my dad started, just as the walkie-talkie on the captain's desk started crackling.

The captain held up a hand as if to say *Just a minute*, and picked up the walkie. "Yes?" he asked, and as I watched, his expression grew more grave. "Uh-huh," he muttered, turning away from us and holding the walkie up to his ear so we couldn't hear anything being said by the person on the other line—just the sound of static. "Okay," he said as he turned to us again and set the walkie back down on his desk. "We're going to need to revisit this another time. Right now I need all of you back on deck as quickly as possible."

"What's going on?" Karen asked, clearly picking up—like I had—on the captain's tone, which was grave and no-nonsense . . . the way you sounded when something was really wrong.

"This boat is going back to shore immediately," the captain said as Hallie and I got to our feet. "All nonessential emergency boats have been ordered to return to shore."

"Um," I said, wondering if there was something I'd missed. "Why?"

"We just got a report from the National Weather Service," the captain said, his voice more serious than ever. "We need to get back to shore ASAP. There's a major storm front bearing down on the Hamptons."

I glanced over at Hallie, meeting her eyes just as the first clap of thunder sounded.

CHAPTER 2

"**W**ow," Sophie said from the backseat, her voice worried. "It's really coming down out there."

I looked out the window and then across Bruce's SUV at my dad, and folded my arms over my chest. The storm the captain had warned us about didn't really seem to be happening—to me, it didn't look like anything more than heavy rain with occasional flashes of lightning and rumbles of thunder. It really seemed like every other summer storm, *maybe* a tad heavier than usual, but not by much. I honestly wasn't sure this whole thing hadn't just been a ploy by the captain to bring in the boat early and get us all off his ship. "Uh-huh," I said a moment too late. If I'd been answering anyone else but Sophie, I would have worried I was being incredibly rude, but she'd been my best friend pretty much all my life, and I knew she would forgive me for being distracted.

During the year, Sophie lived in Putnam, Connecticut, like me. But she'd shown up in the Hamptons earlier this summer, needing a distraction after a bad breakup, and had ended up staying and then babysitting the world's least likable twins. She'd gone to Hallie's party with Reid Franklin—Josh's roommate from boarding school who was spending the summer with him after he'd been fired from his internship—but in the confusion of everyone hustling off the boat and getting into their cars at the marina, she'd walked over to my car, probably out of habit, and ducked in before the rain got really bad. My dad had also headed over to the SUV after a quick, whispered talk with Karen. Since I hadn't even been aware he'd been in this time zone, let alone this state, I had no idea how he'd gotten to the boat in the first place. But when he held out his hand for my keys, it was clear he was coming back to Bruce's with us—and he'd be doing the driving.

A lot had happened quickly when we were hustled out of the captain's quarters—the embers of the party were pretty much squelched out when the announcement came over the PA system, warning there was a storm approaching and there were life jackets available for guests who wished to wear them. I saw Hallie rolling her eyes at me as I took one and belted it around my waist, but I didn't care. It wasn't that I thought some massive storm was going to hit us—though it did, in fact, look like all the other boats around us during the party were making their way in as well—but that I wasn't entirely sure Hallie wouldn't shove me overboard if she got the chance. I also wasn't entirely sure Gwyneth wouldn't do the same thing and tell me it was Hallie, just to give her documentary a little extra excitement.

But the life jacket had somehow come with me in the confusion, and it was now sitting in the backseat next to Sophie, who was keeping up a mostly one-sided conversation about the weather, clearly trying to mitigate some of the silent, angry vibes flying back and forth between my dad and me.

Though we hadn't said anything to each other beyond the basic rudimentary topics about the weather and the best route home, I could sense the tension brewing between us. And it wasn't just that I was mad at my father (which I was). It was also that he was mad at *me*, and I could practically feel it coming off him in waves.

"Sure is," my dad said in response to Sophie, his voice flat, as he turned the wiper speed up. It *did* look like the rain was starting to come down harder now, I had to admit. But it still didn't look like anything worth hauling in a boat over.

I squinted out the rain-streaked window, trying to get a sense of where we were. I wanted to go home and change out of this dress and wash my hair until I was sure there was absolutely no frosting left in it. But mostly, I wanted to not be in this car anymore, confined with my dad, both of us mad at each other.

"When we get back," my dad said, hitting the turn signal with a little more force than was probably strictly necessary, "we're going to call your mother. I don't care if she's in Scotland. She needs to know what you've been up to this summer."

I felt a dull heat creep into my cheeks. "Sure," I said, trying to keep the anger I was feeling out of my voice. "Hey, while we're at it, why don't we also tell her you decided to get *engaged* without even talking to me about it first? Or, you know, even telling me you were dating someone?"

"Oh, look," Sophie said, her voice straining to be cheerful. "A traffic jam."

"That is not the issue here," my dad said, but I could tell he sounded rattled.

"I think it is," I snapped.

"So I'm just going to put on my headphones," Sophie said as I glanced behind me and saw she was putting her earbuds in. "Not going to be able to hear anything that's happening, that's for sure!" She turned and stared out the window, and I was pretty sure she wanted to be out of this car just as much—if not more—than I currently did.

"I just . . ." I started, then took a breath. While I was pretty sure Sophie could probably hear what was happening, despite the sound of her music coming through her headphones, I needed to get this out. "I just don't understand why you wouldn't tell me something like this," I said, hearing in my voice the hurt I wasn't able to keep hidden. As I spoke, I realized it wasn't just about this—although this was a big part of it. It was about this whole summer, and how I hadn't felt like I could talk to him about what was happening. It was about how I'd realized, in the last two months, that my dad and I stuck to the surface, neither of us going too deep or sharing too much. And that had been fine, or at least not as noticeable, when I'd only seen him on vacations and holidays, a few months a year. But living in the same house with him all summer, neither one of us telling the other the truth . . . it was harder to ignore. And I really didn't like it.

"I tried," my dad said after we'd driven in the rain, in silence, for a few moments. "I asked how you would feel if I started dating someone."

"Yes," I said, feeling my frustration start to rise again, "but you said it like it was a hypothetical. Not like it was already happening!"

I let out a breath, trying to get control of my emotions again. I wanted to be able to talk to my dad—just like I'd wanted to tell him, five years ago, how much it had hurt me when I'd found out he was secretly seeing Karen. And how maybe all this—including where I'd ended up, in my ripped dress and frosting-covered hair—could have been avoided if we'd just told each other the truth.

My dad swung into Bruce's ridiculously long driveway, and I had to squint through the rain just to see the house in the distance. Bruce's mansion was large enough as to make no sense whatsoever, and you usually didn't have trouble spotting it—quite the opposite, in fact. When I couldn't see it right away, I realized just how hard the rain had started to come down—and finally conceded that maybe the captain was on to something after all.

"Oh, look—the house," Sophie said, sounding beyond relieved as my dad pulled the car into the garage. She took her earbuds out, and the car had barely been put into park before she was opening her door and jumping out. "I'm just going to head in. See you guys in there," she said, already speed-walking toward the door, making it abundantly clear just how uncomfortable we'd just made her car ride.

She slammed her door, and my dad cut the engine but didn't make any move to get out of the car, so I stayed put as well. There was silence between us, the only sound that of the garage door swinging shut, muffling the rain coming down hard outside and beating against the roof.

I glanced around. Normally, the garage housed the cars of Bruce and my dad, along with several old bicycles, none of which ever seemed to have quite enough air in their tires. But now there was barely enough room for the SUV, since the garage was currently filled with construction equipment. Bruce had started to build a helipad earlier this summer (despite the fact that he didn't own a helicopter), but work on it had been halted when Teddy had chained himself to a backhoe in protest of the destruction of the habitat of the marsh warbler. And it looked like the garage was where the equipment had been stored in the meantime.

I saw that Gwyneth's hybrid was parked where it always was, next to Bruce's ridiculous sports car—it was bright purple and low-slung, and nobody living in the house (including Bruce) had any idea how to drive it. "Looks like Gwyneth beat us here," I said as I gestured to the car, then realized a moment later maybe she hadn't driven herself over to the party. I'd had no idea she was even going, since she'd kept the fact that she was dating Josh to herself. Though, given that she'd just publicly humiliated his sister at her birthday party, I wasn't sure how much longer that relationship was going to last. But either way, in the hustle of everyone leaving, I'd forgotten about Gwyneth—and suddenly worried she was stranded at the marina, looking for a ride home.

A second later, though, I remembered who I was thinking of. Gwyneth was not the type to get stranded anywhere. She was great at taking care of herself—no matter what the consequences might be for anyone else.

"Looks like it," my dad said, matching my tone, and hearing this, I felt my stomach sink. Was this what we were going to go back to—one moment of getting close to maybe talking about something real only to revert to talking about the most superficial stuff immediately after? Suddenly there was so much unsaid between us, I wasn't even sure how to begin to fix it.

But, I realized a moment later, maybe there was a reason neither one of us was making a move to get out of the car yet. Maybe my dad *wanted* to talk to me about real stuff, wanted to open up, but just didn't know how. And maybe I'd have to be the one to help him get there. "I . . ." I started, then took a big, shaky breath, feeling like we were entering uncharted territory, and I was without a map or a GPS or any kind of guide that would tell me if I were heading in the wrong direction entirely. But I figured there was nothing to do but jump in. "I'm really sorry about everything that happened with Hallie this summer," I said. It was like I was feeling my way along in the dark, not really sure where I was going but just needing to keep moving forward. "And I am *really* sorry for what I did five years ago. I've never stopped being sorry about that. I tried, earlier this summer, to make up for it, but . . ." My voice trailed off as I realized my dad probably didn't need to hear, at this moment, how I'd gone under Sophie's identity to try to make things right with Hallie . . . not knowing, of course, that Hallie knew exactly who I was and was using that to her advantage, extracting her revenge at every turn. I glanced across the car. My dad was looking down at the steering wheel, not speaking, but I could tell he was listening.

I took a breath and went on. "But I guess I never felt like I could tell you about it? And that's not good. I mean . . ." My voice was starting to get shaky, and I drew in a sharp breath trying to gather myself. It was feeling like a lot of old wounds, old hurts, were threatening to rise to the surface, and I pushed back against them as hard as I could, just trying to get through this. "I mean, you're my dad," I said, making myself put a lighthearted spin on the last word, so I wouldn't burst into tears. "And I want us to be able to tell each other everything." I paused then, realizing what I'd just said. "Well, maybe not *everything*," I added quickly. "But more things. Most things. What . . . I mean, how does that sound to you?" I held my breath as I looked over at him, hoping maybe this could be a way forward for us. Because, really, all this—the whole mess with Hallie—had begun when he hadn't told me about Karen. If he had, maybe I wouldn't have acted the way I did when I was eleven. Maybe I wouldn't have spent this whole summer first trying to make things right with Hallie, and then vowing retribution and trying to make her pay. Maybe I could have told him about how the thing I was most afraid of when I'd found out he was first dating Karen—that he'd leave to be with her family and I'd never see him again—had actually come to pass when he'd moved to California and out of my daily life, so I only saw him a few times a year. How I missed him and wanted this—wanted us—to be better.

My dad had been nodding along as I'd been speaking, and now he took a deep breath of his own. "I think . . ." he started, then shook his head. "I think I have to tell you something," he said, and I could hear in his voice that he was nervous, and not like when he was nervous because Bruce was yelling at him about getting his draft in on time. Nervous in a real way. "Karen and I," he said, running his hand along the steering wheel, then letting out a breath and turning to me. "We didn't get engaged."

"Oh," I said, blinking at him in surprise. I felt myself start to smile, and it was like a weight was slowly lifting off my shoulders, like with every second I was starting to feel a little lighter. "Well, *good*," I said with a small laugh, realizing maybe this whole thing had just been a misunderstanding. After all, they hadn't exactly come out and *said* they'd gotten engaged, had they? Maybe Karen was just into wearing huge diamonds on her left ring finger. I mean, it was possible. I didn't know her life. "That's great," I said, feeling my smile widen, "because—"

"I mean, we didn't get *engaged*," my dad said again, interrupting me. "We got married."

CHAPTER 3

I stepped inside Bruce's foyer, my dad behind me. I looked around, feeling a little numb. Everything appeared just as it had been when I'd left earlier that afternoon—it was a gigantic room, bigger than my bedroom back home, despite the fact that its only purpose was to lead you to the other rooms—the TV room and kitchen off to the left; straight ahead, the grand curving staircase that brought you up to the main bedrooms; and the hallways that led to Bruce's domain—his office, screening room, and brag room, which was basically just a room for his collection of trophies and memorabilia. There was a giant stuffed polar bear in the corner, but even that wasn't weird—it had been there for weeks now, a gift from the studio in an attempt to convince my dad to write an animated time-traveling Christmas movie. But despite the fact that everything looked just the same as it had a few hours ago, it felt, by all rights, that it *should* have looked different. When a bombshell that large is dropped, you want to see the effects of it, somehow.

"Gem?" my dad asked as he set his keys on the console table (something we were never allowed to do when Rosie, Bruce's longtime assistant, was in town), and started to head toward his office. "You . . . okay?"

I nodded, but even as I did, I was wondering why I was making that movement with my head. I was *not* okay. I hadn't been okay since my dad had told me he and Karen were now *married*. I think he'd expected me to, but I hadn't asked any follow-up questions, hadn't pressed him for any details. Because if I did that, this was real. And my dad had married Karen Bridges without talking to me about it first, without even telling me they were dating again. And that was something I just wasn't feeling up to handling at the moment.

"Well . . . okay," he said, taking another step away, though I could sense his hesitation. "But if you want to talk or anything, I'll just be in there. And we should see about dinner soon."

"Dinner," I repeated, and I could hear how flat my voice was sounding. "Right. Sure." I looked down at the marble floor, wondering if my dad was picking up on how not okay with this I was. And maybe he was, but he didn't seem to care, as he just nodded and headed back down the hall to his office, the door shutting with a small click.

I looked around the empty, quiet foyer. I could hear the sound of rain beating down on the roof above me. It had rained this summer, but I didn't think I'd ever heard it quite this loud before. Maybe it was because there was nobody rushing through, making noise, so the only sound I could hear was the rain on the roof and the occasional rumbles of thunder in the distance.

I could feel a dangerous, restless energy in my chest, like I was about to do or say something I knew I'd later regret but wasn't going to be able to stop myself from doing or saying. I knew I'd felt this way before, but I couldn't put my finger on exactly when. Feeling like I should probably not be around other people right now, not when I was feeling so out of control, I headed up to my room, taking the steps two at a time.

Twenty minutes later I'd showered and changed out of the party dress that, unfortunately for Bruce's ex-wife, I had a feeling was now ruined. But I figured, as I headed back downstairs, if she really cared about it, she would have come back to get it sometime in the last three years.

I had somehow hoped my shower would have magically made things better, but as I passed my dad's office door, I could feel all the same feelings rushing back again at full force. And just like that, I knew when I'd felt this same way before. It was five years ago. It was the moment I'd found out about my dad and Karen. The moment that everything had changed.

I had the same upset, churning feeling happening now. The same recklessness, the same willingness to forge ahead and forget about the consequences. But it was even worse now, because what had just happened was definitive proof that *nothing* had changed in the last five years. My dad was still making decisions that would impact my life, but not telling me about them. We were still keeping secrets from each other. We were right back where we'd been—except it was somehow worse this time around.

I took a half-step toward my dad's door. I wasn't really sure what I was going to say to him, but I knew I had to say something. I didn't think I could let this go—I didn't think I *should*, not feeling the way I currently was—like I was on the verge of exploding.

"Gem?" I turned around, and there was Ford Davidson, leaning against the doorway that led to the kitchen and giving me one of his half-smiles.

"Hi," I said, taking a step toward him, smiling back automatically. But before I could reach him, a revelation came flooding in. I suddenly remembered what I'd realized on the boat, right before everything had fallen apart. Ford was Bruce's son, and in addition to being a championship surfer, he was a computer genius who went to boarding school in Silicon Valley, along with other computer geniuses. I'd had a crush on him since we were kids, back when he was short and chubby, with thick glasses and headgear. Even though he'd given me my first kiss on my thirteenth birthday, nothing had ever happened between us since. But this summer, post-Teddy and post-Josh, I'd been thinking about Ford a lot more than ever before, and wondering if there could be a real possibility of an us. But even though Sophie had been encouraging me to go for it, I'd held back. Even though it seemed like maybe he was also thinking along the same lines, I'd been terrified I would make a move, he wouldn't feel the same way, and our friendship—which was so important to me—would be wrecked. But then, on the ship, I'd had a realization that had seemed to change everything.

Gwyneth had mentioned Ford's algorithm, the one he'd been working on all summer, the one I still wasn't entirely sure about the function of—his Galvanized Empathic Multipurpose Media Algorithm. We'd been teasing him about it all summer, telling him he needed a different name. And when Gwyneth had mentioned it in passing, it was like something in my brain finally clicked, and I'd realized what it was—what had been in front of my face for weeks now. It was an acronym. It spelled out *GEMMA*.

He'd named it after me.

Only the night before, when Sophie had been asking me why I didn't want to tell Ford how I felt, or make a move, I told her our friendship meant too much to me—I didn't want to do something that might strain or jeopardize it . . . not without some sign he felt the same way. And there had been my sign. I had realized, as I'd stared at the words that spelled out my name, knowing it wasn't a coincidence—Ford was way too methodical for that—that Ford had stood by me through everything. He'd learned about what I'd done to Hallie when we were kids, and he hadn't dropped me as his friend. He'd even helped me during the revenge war, strategizing with me about ideas, but also more immediate concerns, like what to do with the nine hundred dollars of cheese Hallie had sent to the house and charged my dad for. But he had been just as understanding when I told him I wanted to stop. Josh had dropped me the second he'd found out I'd been lying to him about who I was. And I'd never told Teddy about what I'd done when I was eleven, because I had a feeling he'd never see me the same way again. But it had been Ford—Ford, this whole time—seeing me for who I was, flaws and all, and accepting me.

I had realized this back on the boat, and had had my phone

out—I had been about to call him. I hadn't figured out what I was going to say—yet—but I'd known then he was the only person I wanted to talk to. But that was just before the video had started to play, and everything had crashed down around my feet.

But now . . . here was Ford, standing in front of me. Was this my moment? Should I tell him how I felt? Should I at least ask him about the algorithm?

"You okay?" Ford asked, taking a step closer to me, causing my heart to beat harder. I looked up at him—it was still something that occasionally took me by surprise, since for years he'd been shorter than me—at his black-black hair sticking up in little spikes, his tan skin, his hipster-cool glasses. He was *Ford*; he was someone I knew as well as anyone. But the thought of talking to him about this—about moving things into another direction—made me feel like I was looking at a complete stranger. And I was suddenly more nervous around him than I could remember being in a long, long time.

"Yeah," I said, going to smooth down my hair and then realizing it was still wet. I twisted it quickly up into a knot, just to buy myself some time as I tried to figure out if this was my moment. I'd been all ready to call Ford on the phone from the boat, but that had been before my fight with Hallie, before the bombshell my dad had just dropped on me. And plus, there was the fact that this was much harder to do face-to-face. But I wasn't sure this was going to get any easier the longer I put it off. I took a breath. "So . . ." I started just as Ford turned and headed back into the kitchen.

"How was the party?" he asked as I followed, trying not to

jump when a clap of thunder sounded, louder than ever before, making me feel like the foundations of the house were rattling.

"Good," I said automatically, just trying to get myself back into the space where I could maybe think about telling him I was having feelings for him. Ford pulled open the fridge and held out a bottle of water to me, a question in his eyes, and I nodded and took it. "I mean, not good," I amended a moment later, when I realized what I'd just said. "It was pretty bad, actually. Hallie and I got into a fight."

Ford had raised his water bottle to his lips, and he paused it there as he quirked an eyebrow at me. "Well, that's not exactly new," he said.

"No, an *actual* fight," I said, taking a sip of my own water as I gave him the abridged version—Gwyneth going ahead and playing the video anyway, Gwyneth's secret documentary, Hallie's inability to believe me when I told her I wasn't behind it. Ford had taken a seat at the kitchen counter during the retelling of this, and had been listening to me, occasionally shaking his head or grimacing at just the right places.

"Well, she's not going to be able to use any of it," he pointed out as I stopped to take a breath and then a drink of water. "Unless she got releases from everyone on the boat, which I highly doubt."

I nodded. It was cold comfort at the moment, but it was something to know that Hallie and I throwing cake at each other wouldn't be able to be featured in Gwyneth's documentary. "But that's not even the worst of it," I said, feeling my stomach sink as I remembered the reality of what my dad had done.

"It gets worse?" Ford asked, sounding scared, and I nodded.

"Yeah," I said with a grim laugh as the feelings that had been coursing through me earlier threatened to return at full force. It was anger mixed with frustration, and the strength of it scared me. "My dad just told me a few minutes ago. He and Karen—they got *married*." I looked at Ford and waited, ready for him to be just as outraged and angry at this as I was.

But Ford just shook his head. "Man," he said, "I'm sorry about that, Gem. Paul didn't even give you a heads up?" He gave me a sympathetic grimace. "That's rough."

"It's not *rough*," I said, feeling my voice start to rise. "It's . . . I mean, you did hear me, right? My dad got *married*. Behind my back, without talking to me about it first, without even telling me he was dating her."

"I heard you," Ford said, giving me another one of his half-smiles. "But you know my last three stepmothers? Bruce just had Rosie send me an e-mail letting me know I had a new relative."

"That's different," I said immediately, realizing a moment too late that maybe Ford hadn't been the person to talk to about this. Both of his parents had been remarried and divorced countless times, so he was used to this by now.

"How is it *different*?" Ford asked, his voice more quiet, and I suddenly wondered if I'd overstepped.

"No, I mean, it's not," I said quickly, shaking my head. "It's just . . ." I wasn't sure what to say to follow that, and an awkward silence fell between us. And we never had awkward silences. I looked across the kitchen counter at him. Suddenly the thought of bringing up the algorithm, or telling him how

I was feeling . . . this didn't seem like it was the moment. I should have just done it back in the hallway, shouldn't have even hesitated. Because now things were just feeling . . . off between us. I took a breath, to try to set this right again. "All I was trying to say was—"

Before I could continue, the doorbell rang. Ford and I both glanced at the door and then looked at each other. "You expecting anyone?" he asked.

"No," I said as I started to head toward the front door, Ford falling into step alongside me. "You?"

"Nope," he said. "And I really don't know who'd be stupid enough to be out in this weather."

We started across the foyer just as Sophie was coming down the stairs, also having changed out of her party dress, her expression furrowed. "Who's *outside* in this?" she asked. "It's miserable out there."

"It's just a little rain," I said as we headed for the door.

"It's more than a little rain," Sophie said, shaking her head. "Have you looked recently?"

Not answering this, I pulled open the front door and felt my jaw drop in surprise. Standing on the front steps in the rain, all looking unhappy about it, were Karen, Reid, Teddy, Josh, and Hallie.

CHAPTER 4

"**T**his is so weird," Sophie whispered to me ten minutes later as we looked at the unlikely group that had assembled in Bruce's living room. "What is even *happening*?"

"I don't know," I said, shaking my head, still trying to understand how this had come to be. I caught Ford's eye from across the room—somehow he'd gotten pulled into a conversation with Reid, who was talking away at him, gesturing big, not seeming to notice that Ford was moving farther and farther away from him on the couch, clearly trying to make his escape.

When we'd opened the door, I'd just stared at the collective group on the doorstep, all of whom were wet and in formal wear and none of whom looked happy to be there, wondering what this meant. Before I could ask, though, my dad had appeared in the doorway, motioning everyone inside, offering people warm drinks and towels—which seemed a little extreme to me, since they'd only been standing in the rain for a few minutes, not swimming the English Channel or anything. But I had to admit, as I pushed the door closed against the wind that was starting to howl, that Sophie had been right—it was getting pretty bad out there. Even just in the time since my dad had driven us home, the weather seemed to have gotten exponentially worse.

When I'd closed the door and everyone was safely inside, I'd received my answer—this collective group had all taken a car service to the boat, and so had gotten back in it after the party had so abruptly ended. But the storm really must have gotten worse than I'd realized, because the car—which had just been a regular Lincoln Town Car—couldn't get through to Karen's house due to flooding. They'd needed to go someplace so she could get picked up in the SUV the service would send . . . and the closest address was, it seemed, Bruce's.

Everyone had congregated in the living room and was just now waiting for the SUV that was supposedly on its way. But I couldn't stop staring at the group that had assembled, feeling a little bit like I'd just woken up in one of my worst nightmares.

Two of my exes—though I wasn't *really* sure Josh counted, because we'd never been official—were there. Not to mention Hallie, who was still shooting me death glares every few minutes, like she needed to keep me reassured she was still furious at me. The only person in the room who I didn't have some kind of complicated history with was Reid, who was also, incidentally, the only person who seemed happy to be there.

And it was clear, from looking at everyone for a few seconds, it wasn't just me who people were mad at. There were bad feelings flying fast and furious within this group. Hallie and Teddy were huddled in a corner, having what looked like an intense conversation, their voices getting raised occasionally, neither one of them looking very happy, and Josh was sitting on the couch, his arms folded over his chest, occasionally glaring at his sister.

Bruce's giant TV had been turned on to the Weather Channel, but the volume was off, so we were left with images of storm warnings flashing across the screen, and meteorologists in foul-weather gear standing on beaches, holding umbrellas that always seemed on the verge of blowing away. Again, Sophie had been right—while I'd been focusing on the bombshell my dad had dropped, I'd failed to notice that the storm outside had gotten much, much worse—to the point where even the non-weather channels seemed to be covering it. A rumble of thunder shook the house, and the lights flickered for a moment. I glanced out the floor-to-ceiling windows that lined the living room, at the trees being whipped back and forth by the wind, their branches waving wildly, and was suddenly grateful, even though I was surrounded by people I'd rather not be around, that I was inside, and dry. The storm starting to rage outside was looking worse by the minute.

My dad and Karen were standing across the room from me, both of them occasionally sending worried looks at the television as Karen continually called the car service company, trying to get specifics on when their SUV would be coming.

Even though I wasn't sure it was the best idea for me to be near my dad or Karen at the moment—I felt like I was a heartbeat away from turning to both of them and yelling, *What were you two thinking?!*—I was trying to keep an ear out for the car updates, feeling as invested in the answer as Karen was. I was more than ready for everyone who didn't currently live in Bruce's house to leave, and it worried me that, according to the news, roads were getting more treacherous, flooded, and accident-filled by the moment.

"Now I'm not getting any reception," Karen said as she lowered her phone and shook her head. "I just wanted to get an ETA." I saw Hallie and Josh shoot their mother looks that clearly said *Get us out of here*, and Karen turned to my dad. "Is there a landline I can use?"

My dad nodded, motioning for Karen to follow him. "In my office," he said. "This way." They left, and I glanced at Sophie, trying to catch her eye so I could silently get her to leave with me. I mean, did we really have to stay there, in a room where at least half the people were furious at me? I wanted to have some alone time with her anyway, to talk to her about what had happened with my dad and find out what was going on with her and Reid—despite Sophie swearing up and down that he wasn't her type, they'd looked *very* cozy on the boat. But Sophie wasn't looking at me, and when I followed her gaze, I understood why. Reid was walking toward us, smoothing down his hair as he went, and Sophie's smile was getting wider the nearer he got. Ford mostly seemed thrilled to be done with being forced into a conversation with Reid, and he widened his eyes at me from across the room.

"Hi, Sophie," Reid said, and I noticed his cheeks were flushed.

I looked between the two of them, trying to figure out what was happening here. Reid had had a crush on Sophie from practically the moment he'd seen her, but it no longer appeared one-sided, since Sophie was smiling back up at him.

"Reid," she said with her very best patented flirt-giggle. I tried to keep the incredulous expression off my face. Sophie had originally agreed to go with Reid to Hallie's party just to get information—but at some point, when I'd been too wrapped up in my own drama to notice, had her feelings become real?

Reid took his eyes off Sophie with what seemed like real difficulty and then looked at me. "Gemma," he said, his voice getting more serious. "Can I ask you something?"

"Um," I said, feeling my defenses go up. What if he wanted an explanation for what he thought had happened at the party? I racked my brain, trying to remember if he'd been in any of the footage we'd shown. Or maybe he had realized I'd been filming him as well, on the mini-camera I'd been wearing for the last three weeks, and was mad about the invasion of his privacy?

It wasn't like I knew Reid all that well, but we'd worked together at the local ice-cream shop, Sweet & Delicious—or we had, until I'd gotten fired. Was he putting any of it together? All the times I'd arranged for him to be absent so I could scheme against Hallie—or recover from one of her schemes against me? "Okay," I finally said when I realized I hadn't answered him. I braced myself for the worst.

But Reid just smiled at me in his vague, pleasant way. "Where's your bathroom?"

"Down the hall, to the left." This was said, not by me, but by Josh and Teddy simultaneously. They both looked over at each other, surprised, and Teddy narrowed his eyes at Josh. Josh knew where things were in this house from the night he'd spent here when we'd both been recovering from food poisoning (Hallie-induced, I later learned). Nothing had really happened between us at the time, but that didn't mean I hadn't wanted something to. And Teddy, I realized, must have learned the layout of the house from the time he spent in the backyard, chained to a backhoe.

"I, uh . . ." Teddy said, leaving Hallie and walking over to Josh, who stood up from the couch. "I didn't realize you'd been here before."

"Once or twice," Josh said, raising an eyebrow at Teddy. "Back when Gemma and I . . ." He looked over at me, and I felt something in my stomach twist as I watched his expression change, becoming closed-off and unhappy. "Back before I knew she was plotting against my sister," he said, shaking his head at me.

I took a breath, realizing this was probably the easiest way—just tell everyone, all at once, and hope they believed me. "I didn't want you to see that footage," I said, and I was met with skeptical looks from everyone except Sophie and Ford. "Well, initially I did. But then I called it off. Gwyneth went ahead and did it on her own." As I said this, I looked around, realizing I still hadn't seen Gwyneth in all the time I'd been home. Bruce's house was big enough that this wasn't *that* surprising, but I really would have thought I would have at least seen her passing through. I thought back to her car in the garage, wondering again if she'd even driven. Maybe my assumption that she'd been here this whole time had been off from the beginning.

"The video was very *illuminating*," Teddy said, his voice cold as he looked right at Hallie. "Things I wish I'd known earlier. Like that my entire relationship was a sham—"

"Teddy," Hallie interrupted him, her face turning bright red as she looked at all of us. She walked closer to him and lowered her voice, but I could still hear every word. "Can we talk about this in private?"

"I don't think so," Teddy said, taking a step back from her, shaking his head. "Why would you think I'd want to talk to you after what I was just shown? Are you crazy?"

"Hey," Josh said, taking a step toward Teddy, his expression serious. "Don't talk to my sister that way."

"Josh, I can handle myself," Hallie snapped.

"Oh really?" he asked, turning to her. "Like how you can lie to me for the last five years? Watching that video, it was like I don't even know you anymore."

"Well, whose fault is that?" Hallie asked, and I could hear her voice was shaking—though with anger or suppressed tears, I wasn't sure. She pointed at me, her eyes narrowing. "Who do we have to thank for that?"

Hallie, Teddy, and Josh all looked at me, and I took a breath to try to defend myself just as Teddy spoke again. "The problem isn't that I saw you say those things," he snapped. "The point is that you said them!" It seemed like the fight was starting in earnest again, and I took a small step back, hoping to be left out of it for the time being.

I exchanged a look with Sophie, and I saw Ford getting out of the line of fire and coming to join us at the back of the room. "So," Ford said, nodding toward Josh, Hallie, and Teddy, who were starting to argue again, everyone talking over each other. "You know when I said you should feel free to let your friends hang out here whenever?"

"Ha-ha," I said a little hollowly. "They're leaving soon," I added, crossing my fingers as I said it, hoping it would be true. "Don't worry."

Ford just raised an eyebrow at me and then nodded toward the window, where the storm seemed to be getting worse than ever. "You sure about that?"

I looked around, feeling my stomach sink, worried that the answer was getting closer to no with every passing minute.

"Also," Ford said, pulling out his phone and frowning down at it, "where the heck is my sister?"

"I just don't know why you didn't tell me the truth!" I saw that Hallie and Teddy were back to talking to each other, although *fighting* might have been a better word. Looking from one to the other, I couldn't help thinking that this looked like the beginning of a breakup if I'd ever seen one.

"Because," Hallie said, taking a glance back at the rest of us before lowering her voice again. "Because at first I didn't realize . . . I didn't know . . ."

"Whoa." Reid had returned from the bathroom, and I looked

over to see his eyes were wide as he watched the drama unfolding. "How long was I gone?"

Ford looked at Reid and seemed to pale slightly, then walked around the group to stand right next to me, clearly worried about getting caught in another conversation with him.

"Safer over here," Ford said quietly, leaning down to whisper in my ear, his breath against my neck.

"Uh-huh," I managed, concentrating on staying upright and sounding as normal as possible. But I was suddenly all too aware of how close to me he was standing, and how I could have leaned over and rested my head against his chest. I swallowed and blinked hard, forcing myself to concentrate on what was happening and where I currently was. But I knew, just from the fact that I was losing the ability to speak and think clearly while standing this close to him, that I would have to tell him, sooner or later, how I felt. The GEMMA thing was practically an open invitation, and I shouldn't have let the weird vibe between us earlier stop me.

"I can't trust you!" Teddy yelled, and I saw something in Hallie's face crumple—like the confident mask she always wore was starting to slip away. "How can I ever trust you again? Everything you told me was a lie."

"No," Hallie said, shaking her head, wiping tears away as they fell, and I looked down at my bare feet and their chipped polish, suddenly feeling like I was seeing something I really shouldn't see.

"It was," Teddy said, his voice getting low and serious. "You *know* how much I value honesty. It's one of my core belief systems. And you violated that right from the beginning. What does that say about you? What does it say about *me*, that I didn't even see it?"

"I just . . ." Hallie said, her voice shaking as she looked at all of us, then back at Teddy, lowering her voice slightly, but not enough that we all still couldn't hear her. "I just think, if you listened to me—if we could talk this out—"

"There's no point," Teddy said, and I could hear the decisive note in his voice. Teddy was incredibly stubborn, and he usually believed he was right—which was why when he made up his mind about something, it was almost impossible to get him to change it. I'd had two years' experience with this and knew it all too well. "Hallie—we're so done. This is over."

"What?" Hallie asked, her voice breaking. "Teddy—"

"Hey," Josh said, standing up and pointing the remote at the TV, cranking up the volume. I leaned forward to see a reporter in foul-weather gear standing on what I was pretty sure was a beach—but the rain and wind were intense enough that it was difficult to tell.

"There is a *major* storm bearing down on the Hamptons and outlying areas," the reporter was saying, almost yelling to be heard over the sound of the wind. "This is a severe storm warning. We will be watching this closely, since there is a strong chance this could turn into a hurricane."

"Wait, what?" Sophie asked, leaning closer to the TV. Nobody was talking now—aside from Hallie's sniffling, the TV was the only sound in the room.

"Please, for your safety, do *not* venture out into this. We're recommending that everybody stay in their homes. I repeat—for the foreseeable future, please stay where you are."

I looked around the room, feeling my stomach plunge again, seeing the horror I was feeling reflected in everyone's expressions.

This could *not* be happening.

CHAPTER 5

It was happening.

"Okay," my dad said to me through the walkie-talkie over long bursts of static. "How's everyone doing?"

I took a breath and then let it out before I allowed myself to reply. "Well . . ." I said as I looked around. Almost everyone was hunched over their phones, fights having stopped and everyone retreating to their separate corners, trying to find a way out of there and looking for proof that this news report could be something other than the truth. Everyone looked more miserable than before—except Sophie and Reid. Reid, upon hearing he was going to be stuck in the same house as Sophie—possibly overnight—had been practically humming.

My dad and Karen had returned from my dad's office to find all of us staring in horror at the television. It turned out that the car Karen had thought was coming was stuck on the side of the road with a blown-out tire, and it was clear it wouldn't be coming anytime soon. Even if the tire somehow got fixed—in the pouring rain—the news was also reporting on all the roads that were currently being closed, one right after the other, until it seemed like there was really no way out of the Hamptons, not without a helicopter or a submarine. Unlike the rest of us, my dad seemed to accept the fact that we were all marooned here, and he'd jumped into action, along with Karen. They got guest rooms organized (not hard in Bruce's mansion, which had way too many rooms to make any logical sense, most of which I'd never even been in) and had unearthed a set of walkie-talkies from Bruce's office. My dad had given one to me, since cell reception was getting worse by the minute. Then he and Karen had gone off to set up the guesthouse for themselves. I was just pretending all the setting up of rooms was just precautionary, just for people to have places if they needed some alone time. I really wasn't letting myself accept the fact that I might be stuck here, overnight, with Hallie, Josh, and Teddy (Reid, I didn't really mind so much). And it was clear everyone else pretty much felt the same way—they seemed to be in collective denial, trying to find a way out of this.

Ford had started to get seriously worried about Gwyneth's whereabouts the longer we went without hearing from her, and he'd texted her until he'd gotten a response. She'd texted back that she was in the middle of something, but okay, and would call soon. "What could she be in the *middle* of?" Ford had asked me, sounding incredulous. "There's a hurricane out there!"

Now my walkie crackled with static, and I lifted it to my ear. "Gem?" my dad asked.

"Right," I said, pressing the button on the side, realizing I'd left him hanging. "Uh . . . I guess it's going okay."

"Hey, I think I might have gotten a taxi," Teddy said, hunched over his phone. "It could be here in an hour, and . . ." His face fell. "Oh, it's not a hybrid."

"Even if you could get a taxi, they've closed most of the bridges," Ford said as he looked up from his spot on the couch, where he had done something to Bruce's flat-screen so it was showing five news reports at once. Ford was probably used to it, since he was always coding using multiple monitors, but it was making me a little bit dizzy to keep looking between the images. "I think we're all stuck here for the moment."

"Well, I need you to help out," my dad said to me, static cutting in every other word. "Get all the supplies you can from the garage. We'll be back to the main house soon."

I heard the *we* in there, and felt myself gripping the walkie more tightly. The arrival of the unwanted guests and the sudden danger of the storm had meant I hadn't had an opportunity to talk to my dad—but I wasn't sure what I would say even if I got one. I still couldn't seem to get beyond my anger about this—and how blindsided I felt. And the same feeling I'd last had when I was eleven, the unshakable belief that something had to be done about this.

"Okay," I said, and waited for another moment, but I heard only static—my dad was no longer on the other end. I set the walkie down on the hall table, glancing out toward Bruce's backyard for just a second. I hadn't spent much time in the guesthouse, since it hadn't really seemed necessary, considering there were more rooms than I knew what to do with *inside* the house. It was on the edge of Bruce's property, and not exactly close—Bruce's property was huge, over ten acres, and the guesthouse was all the way at the back of it. You couldn't even see it from the main house, and it wasn't an inviting walk even when it *wasn't* raining—so I was pretty sure my dad and Karen were going to be soaked through by the time they got back here.

I looked around the living room, at the increasingly dire reports from all the different reporters on the television, and suddenly wished Bruce and his longtime assistant, Rosie, weren't currently in Los Angeles. Bruce wouldn't be much use in this situation—beyond trying to develop it into some kind of disaster movie, no doubt getting people working on a treatment before the rain had even stopped—but Rosie was the kind of person you wanted around in a crisis. She would have handled everything by now—she probably even would have found a way to get the people who clearly didn't want to be here home again. Rosie could work absolute miracles—I'd seen it happen.

"Anyone want to help me get supplies?" I called a little halfheartedly, and wasn't surprised when nobody jumped up to help. I knew if I asked Ford specifically, he would have. But at the moment he was staring at the TV, and I wasn't even really sure he'd heard me. And even though I wanted to talk to Ford—sooner rather than later—I wasn't sure I wanted to try to do it when he was fixated on the Weather Channel. "Okay then," I said with a sigh as I headed off to the garage.

When I stepped inside, I closed the door behind me and leaned back against it for just a moment, realizing the silence was actually a nice change after the yelling and then the strained silences of the TV room. I turned the lights on, and was happy to see they came to life right away—I was trying to tell myself that the flickering a few moments ago was just a one-off thing. But even so, my dad insisted we had to be prepared—which was why I was in the garage. I gathered up flashlights and lanterns, and I found a box of vanilla-scented jar candles, all engraved with the words *New Beginnings*. I stared at the candles for a good five minutes before I realized they must have been left over from one of Bruce's weddings.

My dad had asked me to see if there were any sandbags, but I couldn't find any, which seemed like really bad news to me, considering Bruce's house was right on the beach. It had been one of my favorite things about Bruce's place, but now it was seeming like not such a good idea to have put the house there—particularly if the flooding all five news channels kept reporting on was going to continue happening.

I had just gathered up an armful of supplies—it looked like I was going to have to make two trips to get them all back to the house—when I heard my name.

"Gemma?" I jumped, and three of the flashlights I'd had in my arms went flying, rolling across the garage floor and under what looked like some kind of a crane. I whirled around and saw Teddy standing in the doorway.

"Hi," I muttered as I set down the rest of the things I was carrying on the workbench and then went to go look for the flashlights.

"You okay?" he asked, taking a step farther into the garage.

"Sorry if I scared you." He looked around, squinting at the construction equipment. "Hey, my backhoe," he said, looking across the garage.

I picked up one of the flashlights and winced when I saw that the glass was cracked—meaning we were down one, and it wasn't like we'd had all that many to begin with. "Oh," I said, straightening up as I went to go find the other two, suddenly remembering what had just happened back in the house. "Um . . . sorry about you and Hallie." I stopped immediately after speaking, going over what I'd just said—a sentence I never would have expected to say a few weeks or months ago. But, I realized a moment later, it wasn't untrue. I *was* sorry—maybe because getting broken up with in front of a roomful of people had to be terrible, probably almost as bad as getting dumped in the gardening aisle of Target.

I straightened up and then took a step back when I realized Teddy was much closer to me than I'd expected him to be. "Are you?" he asked, his voice lower than it normally was. "Are you really sorry we're not together anymore?" He looked at me closely, his eyes not leaving mine.

I just blinked at him for a second. I was about to ask what was going on with him, when I suddenly remembered what had happened on the boat. Teddy had come up to me, looking much more confused—and more unsure—than I was used to seeing him. Teddy had always been beyond confident—it was one of the things that had appealed to me so much when we'd first started dating. Teddy knew exactly who he was and how he felt about things—it didn't matter if the issue was saving the marsh warbler or what movie he thought we should see that weekend. He always acted with conviction, which was why it had unnerved me to hear him sound so unsure. But what he said next had thrown me for even more of a loop. He told me he'd been thinking about me, and wondered if he'd made a mistake in breaking up with me—if we should think about getting back together.

It was exactly what I would have given anything to have heard him say—six weeks ago, before he'd totally turned my life upside down.

In the moment when I'd looked at him on the boat, though, I'd realized I wasn't even tempted by this offer. The Gemma who had been with Teddy was someone I didn't even recognize anymore.

But now I realized I'd never actually answered him—and Teddy, based on the way he was looking at me, hadn't forgotten about this.

"Because, Gem," he said, running his hand through his hair and pulling on the ends, the way he only ever did when he was really stressed out, "now that I'm single, I was thinking . . . you know, maybe . . ."

"You've been single," I said, incredulous, "for *maybe* twenty minutes. Are you kidding me?"

"Um," Teddy said, and I saw him deflate slightly, his shoulders hunching. "I don't know. . . ."

"Teddy," I said, shaking my head as I went to find the last

two flashlights. They'd cracked too, so I put them back on the shelf and realized we now had only one flashlight. But that didn't mean there might not be others in the house somewhere. I decided the best course of action might just be to tell everyone that there had only been one in the garage—and hope nobody asked any questions.

"What?" he asked, staring down at the floor of the garage, his expression slightly petulant.

"I just . . ." I said as I looked at him for a long moment. I was trying to recall the guy I'd been so taken with two years ago, the one who seemed to have all the answers, but it was getting harder and harder to make him out. "It's like I don't even know you anymore," I said.

Teddy looked up at me, his brow furrowing. "But you do, Gem; that's the thing," he said, taking a step closer to me. "Like I said on the boat, I feel like I haven't even been myself since we broke up. I mean, I sold Bruce my life rights so he could destroy the habitat of the marsh warbler. Who *does* something like that? Who have I become?"

"Um," I said, feeling my eyes widen. Teddy seemed to be spiraling, which I'd seen only once, on election day, when he was certain he was going to lose the junior class presidency, which he later won by a landslide.

"But if we were still together, that wouldn't have happened," Teddy went on, and I frowned, not at all following the train of thought that had led him there. "I'd still understand myself. I wouldn't have let myself get dazzled by someone who was only looking out for herself. . . ."

"We were together when you got *dazzled* by her," I pointed out, hearing my own voice rise.

"Oh," Teddy said more quietly now, nodding a few too many times. "Right. Never mind about that one."

"I actually don't think this has anything to do with me," I said a moment later, a little more gently. Yes, Teddy had cheated on me. He'd broken my heart. But I was totally over him now, and all that was left were lingering friendship-type feelings (because it wasn't as simple as friendship yet. Maybe just friendship-adjacent) for someone who'd once meant a lot to me. "I think . . . maybe this is about you."

Teddy blinked at me. "You're right," he said, a note of surprise in his voice. "I need to figure out how this all went wrong."

"Okay," I said, picking up an armful of supplies and gesturing to Teddy to take some. "So, while you're doing that, want to help me out?"

"It's like I need to take a walkabout," he said, talking over me. "Or a vision quest . . ."

"Well, there's an almost-hurricane going on," I pointed out as I gave up and grabbed the rest of the supplies myself. "So I don't think a walkabout is going to happen anytime soon."

"Oh," Teddy said, and his shoulders slumped even farther. "I just need . . . someplace I can get centered again. Someplace where I can find the real me . . ."

"Um," I said as I pushed open the door with my foot, as my arms were full and Teddy wasn't making a move to help. "I'm pretty sure Bruce has a meditation room somewhere on the second floor. But—"

"Perfect," Teddy said, nodding and walking past me, leaving me to turn off the light with my shoulder. "Thank you, Gemma. I shall return when things are as they should be."

"Wait, Teddy—" I called after him, but he was already disappearing down the hall and heading up to the second floor, taking the steps two at a time. I rolled my eyes and then headed back across the foyer, dropping the supplies on the kitchen island and looking a little worriedly out at the weather, which seemed to be getting worse by the minute. I squinted at the rain to try to see if it looked like the ocean was starting to get closer to the house, but I could barely make out anything in the stormy darkness.

Then I headed back into the TV room, hoping maybe, somehow, some miracle had been worked while I'd been away, and everyone who didn't normally live here would have figured out a way to leave.

But one glance around the room told me nothing had changed. Everyone was still in the same places I'd left them, but now they all were looking more despondent than before. I took a breath to say something to Sophie, when my phone beeped with a text message, and a second later I heard Ford's phone and Josh's phone beep as well, and I looked down at mine.

Gwyneth Davidson
Hi, babe! Sorry about the thing on the boat.
But when you see the final cut, you'll know it was worth it.
Footage looks insane!! ☺

It seemed like maybe things were getting a little intense,
so I'm hopping on a flight to L.A. now—
got some editing to do. Talk soon! xoxoxo

I stared down at the phone in my hand, trying to get my
head around it—Gwyneth had just made a huge mess and then
left, only telling me after the fact. I shook my head as I read the
message again, wondering why I was surprised—frankly, I probably should have expected this from her. And it did answer the
question of where she was—the longer I hadn't heard from her,
and the more the storm raged on, the more worried I'd started
to get, even though I was still furious with her.

"You get a message from Gwyn?" Ford asked, looking over
the couch at me.

"Yeah," I said, holding up my phone. I shook my head.
"Apparently, she's skipping town."

"What?" Hallie asked, her jaw dropping. "She just *left*?"

"Had to go back to L.A.," Josh said, disbelief in his voice as
he looked down at his own phone.

"Wait," Ford said, sitting up straighter, some of the laid-
back surfer cadence leaving his voice as it became sharper and
big-brother protective. "Why is my sister texting you?"

"Oh," Josh said, swallowing and then looking at Ford, like he
was only now noticing how tall and in shape he looked. He cleared
his throat and then said, a little haltingly, "Well—Gwyneth
and I, we're actually—"

"They're dating," I said, taking pity on Josh, who looked

beyond uncomfortable as he stumbled through this explanation.

"Oh, *you're* the guy," Ford said, understanding dawning in his eyes. He turned to me, no longer protective, just thrilled with his victory. "Didn't I tell you there had to be a guy?"

I nodded. "You did," I said, trying to match his triumphant grin with a smile of my own. When Ford and I had been speculating that there was someone Gwyneth was secretly dating—or at least crushing on—it had just been fun, since the last person I would have expected her to be dating was Josh. But unless Ford had picked up on what Josh had said earlier—or almost said—he hadn't known about our history. And then a moment later I wondered if what Josh and I had even *counted* as history— what was it called when you had a crush on someone, made out with them once, and then there was nothing except the possibility of a kiss in an ice-cream freezer?

"Wait, how did Gwyneth get on a plane?" Sophie asked the room in general.

"She probably went to the airport," Reid said helpfully from the couch.

"No, it's a good question," Josh said as he pointed to the TV. "I thought I saw they were grounding all the planes."

Ford shrugged and shook his head. "Gwyneth has a way of getting what she wants," he said, and without being able to help it, my eyes darted toward Josh. "No doubt she got on the last one out. She's got good luck that way."

"But . . ." Sophie said, and I could see her brow was

furrowed—she was clearly still trying to get this to make logical sense.

"I just can't believe she would leave like this," Josh said hollowly as he sat down on the arm of the couch, staring at his phone. "I mean . . . she pulls a stunt like that at Hallie's party and then just leaves without even talking to me?"

"It's not really personal," I said, walking over to the couch and sitting next to Sophie. Josh shot me a skeptical look, and I went on, "It's just Gwyneth. She does this sometimes." It was more than sometimes, but I didn't think Josh would really find that information helpful at the moment.

"It's true," Ford said as he came to sit on the couch that faced me. He leaned forward, smiling at me. "Remember when she told us all she was going to make dinner? She'd just watched a *SuperChef* marathon, I think."

I nodded, a hazy memory starting to come back into focus. "When we were, like, thirteen?" I asked, and Ford nodded. "Yeah, so we came back from the beach to find Gwyneth gone, the kitchen a disaster, no food, and a note saying she actually got bored halfway through cooking and we should get pizza instead."

Ford laughed, shaking his head. "And it turned out she'd been hiding the whole time in my dad's office, just waiting for everyone to either stop being mad at her or go to bed, whichever came first."

I found myself laughing as well, but this died down as I looked around the room. We weren't thirteen anymore, and this wasn't about not cleaning up the kitchen. There were actual consequences here, and she had shown the video on the boat, knowing there would be. To leave after that, assuming the rest of us would just deal with it . . . I shook my head. "I know this is what she does," I said to Ford. "But to make this big a mess, deliberately, and then not have the courage to face the consequences . . ."

There was a loud, sharp laugh from across the room, the kind of laugh that was designed to show you actually *don't* find something funny. I looked over and saw Hallie staring at me in disbelief. "Are you actually saying this right now? Are you really that unaware?" she asked.

"What are you talking about?" I asked. She took a step toward me, and I stood up. Hallie looked upset enough that I could feel my heart start to beat harder, like my body was preparing me for conflict, for fight or flight. And right now it looked like Hallie was choosing fight. It hit me just then that we'd never actually resolved the fight we'd had on the boat, the one that had devolved into cake-throwing and shoving. It had been interrupted by our parents and all their revelations. But now it was like everything was coming back at full force, like we'd just had a time-out we'd both agreed was now over.

"Seriously?" she asked, her voice sharp, and the heads of everyone else in the room whipped back and forth as they looked from me to Hallie, like this was a particularly intense tennis match. "So Gwyneth creates a giant mess, spills all kinds of secrets, and then doesn't even have the courage to stick around and face her consequences. Because she's that much of a coward."

Hallie just stared at me, anger and contempt mingling in her expression. "Remind you of anyone?"

I felt heat flood my cheeks as I understood she was talking about me. And then I felt doubly embarrassed when I realized I wasn't sure which time she was talking about . . . what I'd done when we were eleven, or when I'd fled back to Connecticut last week, rather than sorting out the mess my life here had become. "I came back," I said, standing up straighter and walking over to her. "And I never intended for you to see that video—"

"Oh, who cares about the video?" Hallie snapped. "You always have an excuse, don't you?" Hallie asked, her voice getting more and more angry as she took another step closer to me. "It's always something with you." She raised her voice, making it high-pitched and whiny. *"It wasn't me, it was Gwyneth. I was just eleven, I didn't know any better. I was lying for a good reason, I promise."*

"It's not the *best* Gemma impression," Ford said faux-thoughtfully, and I knew he was trying to distract me, lighten the mood, but it really seemed like things had gone too far for that.

"Don't pretend you're so innocent in this," I said, hearing the anger in my own voice increase as I took a step closer to Hallie as well. I wasn't about to let her rewrite history—either of this summer or of the five years preceding. "There was nothing in that video you didn't actually say or do. You might not like admitting the truth, but—"

"The *truth*?" Hallie yelled, and I could see it in her face— this was a fight that had been a very long time brewing, and everything was finally coming to the surface. She shook her head. "Do you have any idea what that word even means?"

"I know it means not *pretending* I met someone by accident, when I was planning on using him," I said, and Hallie flinched. "I know it means not framing someone for theft—"

"Wait, what?" Josh asked his sister. He was looking increasingly freaked out. "What is she talking about?"

I took a breath to answer him, but Hallie was already going on. "Oh, so you just *pretended* to be someone else for six weeks, but I should let that go," Hallie said, rolling her eyes theatrically. "You create this crazy web of lies, you hurt my brother—"

"Guys," Josh said, looking very uncomfortable about being dragged into this. "I—"

"Because I wanted to make things right with you!" I yelled at her, as though volume could get this across when nothing else had. "Because I never stopped feeling horrible about what happened when we were kids. Because—"

"Like I can believe anything you say," Hallie said, shaking her head. "Like you're not just saying whatever you need to—"

"No, that's *you*," I snapped, and Hallie's eyes widened.

"I swear to God, Gemma," she said, her voice low and angry, "if you think I'm going to put up with this—"

"Well, you're going to have to learn how to," I snapped, "considering what's happening."

Hallie took a breath, like she was about to hurl an insult back at me, but she stopped, her brow furrowing. "What do you mean?" she asked. "Considering what?"

I blinked at her and then looked across the room to Josh, to see he looked just as confused as Hallie did. I realized with a start that they didn't know. That my dad had told me, but Karen hadn't told her kids yet. Which wasn't really that surprising, since my dad and I had had a moment together, but there had been a number of unhappy people with them in the car the Bridges had come here in. For just a moment I thought about it. I thought about throwing this information, this bombshell, in her face, and watching as she heard the news. But no matter how I felt about Hallie, telling her this felt like a bridge too far. It felt like I was crossing a line I wouldn't be able to uncross. "Nothing," I said, looking down at my hands, but not before seeing Ford's sympathetic grimace—he had, it seemed, been able to read in my expression exactly what I'd stopped myself from saying.

"Not nothing." This was Josh who'd spoken, to my surprise. He'd stood up and was crossing the room toward me, his eyes searching mine. "You were about to say something, Gemma. What is it?"

"It's *nothing*," I insisted, breaking eye contact and looking down at my bare feet, wishing I hadn't been quite so easy to read—you would have thought after a summer of deception, I would have gotten a little better at it by now.

"Gemma." This was Hallie, her voice low and serious. "Tell me."

I looked between them, and I knew there was really only one thing to do. I wouldn't be telling them to hurt them—I would be telling them because they'd figured it out anyway. "Let's talk in the kitchen," I said, feeling like if I was going to give them the worst news they'd received in a while, they could at least hear it in private.

"Wait, why?" Sophie called, looking crestfallen, as the three of us started to walk down the hallway together. "Come on! We're all, you know, kind of friends here!"

When we made it to the kitchen, I placed myself on the other side of the kitchen island from Josh and Hallie, feeling like some distance might be good if they decided to start throwing things. "So . . . here's the thing," I said, taking a breath, and I told them what I knew, which wasn't much—I hadn't asked my dad any follow-ups, so I basically just knew the bare bones.

"No," Hallie said when I'd finished, and she and Josh had me repeat myself twice. Both of them looked like I felt—like we were all suddenly trapped in one of our worst nightmares together. "They can't have. Not without telling us."

"No way," Josh echoed, shaking his head.

I shrugged. While I wasn't happy they were reacting this way, it at least made more sense to me. Ford's reaction to the news had been so cavalier, it was like we'd been talking about two entirely separate things.

"So we'd be . . . related," Hallie said, pointing between the two of us, her voice laced with equal parts disgust and disbelief. "We'd be . . ."

"Sisters," I finished, shaking my head right after, like that might erase the word.

Even though Hallie didn't speak, it was like I could practically feel her reacting to the word, the shudder she was trying to suppress. "I have to talk to my mom," she said. She looked outside, in the direction of the guesthouse and the torrential rain, and then pulled out her cell phone and walked into the hallway.

"There isn't any reception," I called after her. I took a breath to tell her to use the walkie, but she was already disappearing from view, lifting her phone to her ear.

I looked at Josh across the kitchen island, and for just a moment there was only the sound of the wind howling outside, suddenly seeming much louder than it had before.

I suddenly realized this was the first time we'd been alone since our moment in the ice-cream freezer, our almost-kiss I was now seeing in a totally different light, now that I knew he'd been with Gwyneth while it was happening. But still—there was a piece of my mind I couldn't turn off when I saw him, the piece that reminded me we'd once kissed and it was really, *really* good and we should do it again soon.

"So, um," Josh said, clearing his throat, and crossing and uncrossing his arms. "We'd be related. You and me."

"Um," I said as I felt my stomach turn. "I guess we . . . um, already are?"

Josh paled slightly under his tan, and I realized I felt the exact same way. I'd just had make-out flashbacks with someone who was now, it seemed, my *stepbrother*. I sat down on one of the kitchen island stools, feeling like standing up was getting to be a little too much.

"I can't believe they've done this to us," Josh said a little hollowly. "I mean . . . it's not like this is ever going to work out."

I nodded without looking at him. I'd been upset enough

when my dad had told me, but now the reality was starting to ring more true. This wasn't just about my dad and Karen and my dad not telling me. This was about how he would be forcing me into a family with a person who I hated and who hated me, and another person who I had unsettled, complicated romantic feelings for. As the enormity of it all came crashing down on me, for a moment it was like I couldn't breathe.

"I'm going to try to talk to Gwyneth before she gets on her plane," Josh said, standing up and pulling out his cell phone. I took a breath to say something, but then let it out as I gave up, since apparently none of the Bridges siblings cared to hear that they weren't going to get calls through because the reception was so bad.

I sat alone at the kitchen island, the thoughts swirling in my head starting to move faster and faster. It felt like I was where I was five years ago—except now I was older and, if not necessarily wiser, I at least knew a little more. I knew how to make some things happen. And so did Hallie . . .

The thought made me sit up straight. I dismissed it immediately but then found that it didn't leave quite as quickly as I wanted it to.

"I couldn't get through." I looked up and saw Hallie standing at the other end of the kitchen from me, her arms crossed. I'd been so lost in thought, I hadn't even heard her come back into the room.

There was silence between us, but it was crackling and angry, and I wasn't sure if I wanted to address what was happening, or if I wanted to get back into the argument we'd been having in the captain's quarters before we'd been interrupted. There were so many axes to grind between us, and so many grudges we were keeping, it was almost hard to know where to begin.

"This can't happen," Hallie finally said, breaking the silence.

I nodded. "I know," I said. "I mean . . . *sisters*?" Even the word was enough to make my stomach clench.

"No," she said firmly. "It's pretty much the worst idea I've ever heard."

"Can you imagine?" I said, trying for a laugh, but failing utterly as I thought about what the reality of that might actually mean. Hallie and I, joined together forever at holiday dinners and on vacations. Never knowing if I could actually trust her, always looking over my shoulder, my relationship with my dad wrecked. Being related, even by marriage, to Josh, having to see him and his new girlfriends all the time . . . and the thought that this might be *forever*. That Hallie might be an inextricable part of my life, ruining every holiday and special event into the foreseeable future.

"Actually, I can," Hallie said, and as I looked at her expression, I had a feeling she'd just gone down the same thought process I had (minus the Josh stuff, of course). She turned to me and, mixed with the dawning horror of what our situation might look like, I could see determination in her face. "We have to do something about it."

I paused for a moment before speaking, not knowing if I should tell her I'd just had pretty much the same thought. I wanted to take her word for it, but I knew just what a skilled liar she was, how many times she'd fooled me. *"We?"* I finally echoed, not wanting to put myself out there with a more direct question, only to be shot down.

"We," Hallie said grimly. "It's the only way we're going to be able to stop this."

"Uh-uh," I said, shaking my head. "And what happens when you turn around and stab me in the back? How many times do you expect me to fall for this?"

"Fall for what?" Hallie snapped, narrowing her eyes at me. "I told you before I was done, but then you turned around and stole my job—"

"Oh, don't pretend," I spat, feeling the frustrations of this very long day bubble to the surface all at once, like a pot that had been simmering too long suddenly boiling over. "You told me you were done, and then you turned around and sent your reporter friend here to take a picture of Bruce's award."

Hallie's eyebrows shot up, and she seemed to be genuinely confused. For just a moment I almost believed her, but then I remembered how many other times I'd given her the benefit of the doubt this summer, and how it had always, always come back to bite me. "I have no idea what you're talking about."

"Sure," I muttered, shaking my head. "*Sure* you don't. I'm just saying, I can't trust you. I should have learned it earlier this summer, but I finally know that now. So tell me, why should I suddenly start?"

"Because we want the same thing for once," Hallie said simply. I had a retort all ready to go, but the logic of this made me pull it back and realize—much as I hated to admit it—she was right.

I nodded slowly. "We have to break them up," I said, realizing this was what had been swirling in my head ever since my dad had told me. It was my eleven-year-old plan all over again—except this time, I'd have someone on my side. And this time, it was about the greater good. I wasn't hiding it under the umbrella of doing it for my dad. I would be doing this for me—and Hallie and Josh. I would be doing this so I wouldn't spend my life connected to people who hated me. And I realized I didn't even feel guilty about it. My dad didn't care enough about me to run this past me, or even give me a heads up. Why should I make the same allowance for him? "You're right," I said, the words feeling unfamiliar to me even as I said them.

Hallie looked at me and let out a breath, then crossed and uncrossed her arms. I wondered if she was feeling the same thing I was—that we were now in uncharted territory.

"So . . . we're calling a truce?" I asked, feeling the need to get this out in the open as clearly as possible. Hallie had played me before, and I had no reason to believe she wouldn't do it again.

"I think this is much bigger than our little feud," she said dismissively. I was about to agree with her when something hit me.

"That isn't a yes or no," I pointed out, my voice coming out sharp and spiky. I hated having to do this—hated having to parse every word—but I really felt like I had no other choice. Hallie had driven me to it.

"Hm," Hallie said, one eyebrow raised, and maybe—unless

I was just imagining it—a little more respect in her eyes as she looked at me. "Well, I meant it," she said. "Truce. This," she said, gesturing between the two of us, "is over. For the moment. We have bigger fish to fry. Agreed?"

I looked at her, trying to get my head around the fact that we were now on the same side, united by a common goal that was bigger than both of us. Even as I tried to think about Hallie in this way—not as my enemy, not as someone trying to hurt me, but as someone I was going to need to work with—part of me was screaming that this was a mistake, that Hallie couldn't be trusted, that every time I thought things were different, I got burned. But I swallowed hard and made myself nod. Because I knew, somewhere deep down, Hallie was right. That this *was* bigger than either of us, and I was going to have to put my own feelings, my worries and fears aside, and do the unthinkable—I was going to have to work with Hallie.

"So what do you think?" Hallie asked, and I thought I could hear a note of worry creeping into her voice. I wondered if she was realizing the same thing I just had—if we were going to do this, we were going to do it together. That, like it or not, we needed each other.

"I'll never trust you," I said, looking at her steadily across the kitchen. I didn't want her to think, as she so often had (and not without cause) that I was an easy mark, that I was just going to forgive and forget. I wanted to make sure she knew our wounds went too deep—that no matter what happened here, it wasn't like we were ever going to be BFFs, talking about clothes and fixing each other's hair. It just wasn't going to happen.

"I'll never *like* you," Hallie replied immediately.

"So what's the plan?" I asked, now that this had gotten out of the way, and we were both on the same page. "We break them up?"

"A reverse *Parent Trap*," Hallie said slowly, nodding.

I suddenly flashed back to the summer we were eleven, when we'd watched that movie obsessively whenever there was a chance of a rainy day—she'd preferred the new version; I'd been partial to the original.

I started to take a breath, asking her if she really thought we were capable of doing this, but stopped myself before the words came out. I thought about how Hallie had planned her revenge against me for five years, about how methodically I'd tried to get her and Karen to leave the Hamptons when we were kids. I thought about the escalating war that had consumed both of us for the past few weeks. If anyone could pull this off, we could. It was also the first time it had really hit me—or that I was willing to admit to—just how similar we actually were.

"Shake on it?" I asked, feeling that having Hallie promise not to sabotage me was one thing, but I could use a bit more concrete proof. I suddenly wished I was still wearing one of Gwyneth's cameras. I looked into the living room, wondering if we could ask someone to witness something if we refused to tell them what it was about, or, alternately, if it would be possible to find a local notary in this weather.

Hallie nodded and reached out her hand to me, but then stopped, her hand in midair. "Hey," she said slowly, like she was remembering something from a long way back. "Do you remember that thing we used to say as kids? When we had a really important secret?"

I just blinked at her for a moment, trying to recall this—and then, all at once, there it was. The thing Hallie and I had said to each other when exchanging information about the boys we liked or the secrets we hid from our parents or the things we just wanted to stay totally between us. It had been our catchphrase, and I'd totally forgotten it until right now. "Cross my heart . . ." I started, making the old gesture out of habit.

"Not my fingers," Hallie finished, and we exchanged a tiny smile. Then she held out her hand to me, all the way this time, and I only hesitated for a moment before reaching out.

And we shook on it.

CHAPTER 6

"Wait a second," Ford said, turning to look at me, a piece of cardboard still in his hand, his jaw falling open. "Let me get this straight. You're working with *Hallie*?"

I nodded, going to stand next to him by the window. Ford had been hunched over his laptop from the moment he realized just how bad the storm was getting, learning everything he could about weatherproofing houses. One of the things he'd found across the board was a recommendation that we board up the windows from the inside. We'd glanced around at the mansion and realized that wasn't going to happen, not unless Bruce secretly had a room filled with nothing but cardboard (which, honestly, given Bruce's house, wasn't unimaginable). But since the pool house was the closest house to the water, and its number of windows was manageable, we'd decided to focus on that one.

After Hallie and I had shaken hands, we had both gone our separate ways almost immediately—like we'd both needed a minute to process what we'd just agreed to do. When I'd headed back to the TV room again, the group in the living room had broken up, and it seemed like people were finding the rooms that had been set up for them, maybe finally accepting that nobody was getting out of here anytime soon. It looked like people (the ones who didn't live here) were borrowing clothes—I passed Teddy in the hallway, muttering a mantra, in a T-shirt I was pretty sure was Bruce's, and got a glimpse of Hallie in one of Sophie's dresses. I'd been looking around for Sophie, but carefully—it was like the house had suddenly turned into one of those terrifying haunted houses that pop up around Halloween, but instead of ghosts or vampires lurking around the corners, there were ex-boyfriends and former crushes and Reid. Ford had been the only one still in the TV room, and when he'd told me his weatherproofing plan, I'd immediately volunteered to help—not only because I didn't want all the pool house's windows to shatter, but I figured this might be my moment to tell him how I was feeling, and just hope my algorithm theory was right and he felt the same way. We'd crossed from the main house to the pool house, but this hadn't been the simple trip it normally was. The wind was blowing so forcefully, it was like I could almost feel myself getting picked up off my feet. The wind and rain were whipping across my face so hard, it hurt, and there were giant downed branches everywhere, meaning even though both Ford and I were getting totally soaked, we couldn't run for it, since there was debris blocking our way.

Ford had claimed the pool house as his room for the summer early on, and it was easy to see why—it had its own living room area, with two leather couches that faced each other, and a wall of bookshelves stacked high with paperback thrillers and board games. There was a bed, and its own mini-kitchen and full bathroom. Basically, when I'd seen the pool house, I'd been upset I hadn't called it for myself in the month I'd had here before Ford and Gwyneth had arrived.

When we'd gotten inside, we were both soaked to the bone, and I was shivering in a way that didn't have anything to do with the cold. Because it was really hitting me now—we were stuck in an oceanfront house, in the middle of what was looking more and more like a hurricane. And there was nowhere else we could go, nothing we could do about it.

Well—except board up the windows, which was exactly what we were doing as I told Ford about the developments that had occurred between me and Hallie.

"Hallie," Ford repeated as we tried to fit the piece of cardboard across the window. "You remember Hallie, right? What she did to you?"

I winced. "I know," I said. "But we've put that aside for the moment." Ford shot me a disbelieving look, and I added quickly, "We shook on it and everything."

"I'm not sure it's the *best* idea you've ever had," Ford said, his tone deadpan, and I knew he was understating this for effect.

"I'm right there with you," I said as I took a step back from the window. Ford nodded, and we moved on to the next one. There was another crack of thunder, and I looked outside the glass pool house doors to see a flash of lightning streak across the sky. "But I couldn't see that we had another choice. We have to stop this. I mean . . . Hallie and me as *sisters*?" I asked, not able to stop myself from shuddering. "It can't happen."

Ford just looked at me for a moment, then he silently picked up the next piece of cardboard, turning it in his hands for a moment.

"What?" I asked, when he still didn't say anything. Ford wasn't the only one who could read people—it went both ways, though I wasn't quite as skilled at it as he was. But right now I could tell there was something he was thinking but not telling me.

"You don't have to do this," he said. And just when I opened my mouth to disagree with him, tell him in no uncertain terms that I absolutely *did*, he went on, more quietly, "You could just let your dad be happy." Whatever I was about to say left me as I just blinked at him. "Look, you know how many stepmothers and stepfathers I've had over the years," Ford said, turning from me and working on getting the cardboard to fit in the window. Even though it was pretty dark outside, with the cardboard over the window it suddenly got even darker. "You realize at some point you can't control what your parents are going to do. You just have to make the best of it and hope they're happy for as long as it lasts."

I shook my head. "This is different," I said, knowing even without being able to say why, that it was. "This isn't like when Bruce marries starlets or handbag designers on a whim," I said. "I can't know this will be over in a year at most. I have a history with these people. I can't spend my holidays with *Hallie*. And especially not Josh . . ." The words were out before I could stop them, before I had a chance to think them through. I hoped for just a moment maybe Ford hadn't noticed, that he hadn't been paying attention. But when he glanced over at me, his look was sharp, his eyes behind his glasses missing nothing.

"Why especially not Josh?" he asked slowly. He was looking right at me, and I realized my hope that he hadn't picked up on what Josh had said earlier was in vain—he'd heard exactly what Josh had said. And what was more, he'd understood it.

"Oh," I started, then hesitated. I had never managed to tell Ford about what Josh and I had had earlier in the summer, and it wasn't just because I hadn't found the time. It was because of my crush on Ford, the long-simmering one I'd had since we were kids.

"Gem?" Ford prompted, his gaze right on me, and I dragged myself back to the present moment.

"Right," I said, having to look away from him for just a second before continuing. "So . . . earlier in the summer, before you got here. Josh and I . . . we kind of . . ."

"I see," Ford said slowly, and there was something in his expression that made me wonder if he'd suspected anything before today but had just not said anything.

"Nothing happened," I said quickly, then thought of the one kiss we'd had, the one that still left me dizzy when I thought about it. "I mean, almost nothing. But it was over by the time you got here." Only by one day, but I wasn't sure Ford necessarily needed to know that.

"This is when you were going under Sophie's name?" Ford asked, and I nodded.

"That was kind of what . . ." I said haltingly. "I mean, when he found out who I really was . . ." I let my voice trail off, well aware there was no way to tell someone the details of how you'd been dumped and still retain your dignity.

Ford just looked at me, a small frown between his eyebrows. "Why didn't you tell me?"

"Well," I started, then stopped immediately. I hadn't been expecting this question. And I realized suddenly just how close together we were standing. I looked at him, his dark spiky hair, his hipster glasses with a fingerprint smudge on one of the lenses. I could see his strong arms and shoulders under the Henley he was wearing, and even though they were covered up at the moment, I knew, from a summer of seeing him in his board shorts, just how amazing his abs were. But I also saw the kindness, the steadiness, in the way he was looking at me—no judgment or anger.

Was this the moment? Should I tell him how I felt—that I liked him as more than a friend? That I had for years, but this summer it had become something more?

I looked at him and took a breath, thinking about how to start this, but then lost my nerve. After all, I'd just finished telling him about my history with Josh. What if Ford thought it was the same thing with him—just a passing crush?

And this easy rapport between us—which had always been there, even as my crush had grown over the years—what if it disappeared the second I told him how I felt? What if he didn't feel the same way, algorithm name notwithstanding, and then we had to have the world's most awkward conversation? What if things between us were never the same again? "I don't know why I didn't tell you," I said, hoping my tone was casual and easy, and not letting him know the inner turmoil I was currently going through. I made myself shrug. "I guess it just never came up. . . ." I looked into Ford's eyes and could see the skepticism there. He knew there was something I wasn't telling him; he just didn't know what it was yet. We finished doing the rest of the windows in silence, and it felt to me, with every passing moment, that I'd missed my window to tell him how I felt. There were too many other things swirling in the air now—Josh; my dad and Karen; and Bruce and his myriad exes. It didn't feel right somehow. "So," I said quickly, looking around for something, anything I could use to change the subject as we stepped away from the windows. The whole pool house was much darker now, even though I hadn't thought there was all that much light still outside. But maybe it was the effect of blackout curtains—the near-total absence of light. I saw his desktop computer and the assorted laptops and tablets sitting on his desk, and seized onto that. "How's the algorithm going?"

Ford shrugged and then sat down against the couch, some of his energy ebbing away. "It's working fine," he said, his voice unenthusiastic. "I mean . . . it's okay. But I had much bigger ideas for this algorithm than *fine*, you know what I mean?" I nod-ded, feeling myself smile. Ford was like Bruce in that way—they both dreamed big, leaving the specifics until another time.

"Are you going to change it?" I asked, though even as I said it, I wasn't sure if this was the right terminology. I was pretty sure it wasn't, but I figured Ford would know what I was trying to get at. "Or . . . edit it?"

Ford gave me a half-smile, and I knew he understood what I was saying. "I thought about it," he said. "It would mean doing a lot of rebuilding. Some pretty fundamental pieces would have to be rethought. And I could do that."

"So what's the problem?" I asked, because Ford's tone was indicating he didn't plan on fixing it at all. I sat down across from him, on the opposite couch.

"I don't know," Ford said, letting out a breath. "I've just been wondering if I should leave well enough alone. Maybe it's okay as is. I mean, if something's working fine, why mess with it?"

He looked across the couch at me, and I could feel my heart start to beat harder. I suddenly wasn't sure if Ford was just talking about the algorithm. Was this how he felt about other things? Was this how he felt about *us*—or the possibility of an us?

I suddenly felt my cheeks get hot with retroactive embarrassment. Had Ford been able to pick up on how I was feeling about him? Was this his way of letting me down gently—his way of telling me not to humiliate myself by even bringing it up in the first place? But then, if that were the case, why name the algorithm after me? Before I could begin to sort this all out, Ford stood up, glancing out the pool house door, where the rain was lashing against the windows.

"Well, I'm going surfing," he said, smiling at me. "Want to come?"

"Ha-ha," I said, giving him a smile that then faltered when I saw he wasn't kidding. "Are you *serious*?" I asked, hearing my voice go up about an octave.

"You know I promised to teach you whenever you wanted," he said, his voice overly patient. "Though at this point, I'm beginning to doubt if you'll ever give surfing a try."

"That wasn't what I was talking about," I said. Ford had been trying to get me to surf for years, even offering to give me lessons, but I'd always found an excuse, or told him we'd do it another time. Because navigating the ocean with just a tiny piece of fiberglass had never seemed all that appealing to me. But I didn't care about that now—I cared about the way Ford was looking out at the ocean, like he was actually planning on going out in this.

"What?" he asked, shooting me a grin as he crossed to his dresser and pulled out a pair of board shorts. "What's the big deal?"

"What's the *big deal*?" I echoed incredulously. I pointed outside, where another clap of thunder sounded, practically shaking the foundations of the pool house. "You know how bad it is out there. They were saying on the news that this could turn into a hurricane."

"Exactly," Ford said, smiling at me. "Surfers *live* for weather like this. You know how good the swells are going to be? I've been suffering with your cute little East Coast waves long enough. Time to surf some real waves."

"*No*," I said, horrified, as I began to understand that Ford was actually intending to do this. Bruce and Rosie were gone, and I realized, with my stomach plunging, that I was the only one still there who he might listen to when I told him not to do this. "Ford, please. It's dangerous out there. Tell me you won't go surfing."

"But . . ." Ford said, his eyes sliding outside again, longing in his voice. "Gem, if you just—"

"No!" I said, and the note of fear in my voice took me by surprise—and Ford, too, by the look on his face. "Promise me. Promise me you won't go surfing in this."

"Okay," Ford said quickly, looking a little freaked out. "I promise, Gem. Don't worry."

I let out a long breath, feeling my heart rate start to slow down a little. The thought of him, out in the rain, in the darkness—it had scared me more than I'd been prepared for it to. "Thanks," I said, giving him a shaky smile.

"Here, this might make you feel better about it," he said, extending his pinkie toward me. "I pinkie swear. Okay?"

I smiled as I reached my own hand out. This was how we'd made pacts from when we were around eight on. "Pinkie swear," I said, looping my finger around his. I felt a shiver pass through me when my skin touched his, and I didn't think it was due to the weather outside. Ford looked down at me, not moving his hand away from mine. I was suddenly aware of every centimeter of my little finger, like all my nerve endings were on fire. Was Ford feeling this same way too? Was that why we were still touching?

He looked down into my eyes just as the lights flickered off.

They came back on a moment later, but somehow they weren't as bright as they'd been before.

"Weird," I said, looking up at him, all too aware that we were still touching, still involved in the world's longest pinkie swear.

"Yeah," Ford said, looking down at me, making no move to separate from me. He took a breath, like he was about to speak, when there was a knock on the door. A second later Sophie pushed the door open and stepped inside, looking sodden and worried.

"Hey," she said, her eyes widening as she looked at me and Ford, our hands touching, standing close. "Um. I think there's a problem."

CHAPTER 7

"Okay," Rosie said from the speakerphone in the center of the kitchen island. "Tell me how bad it is."

I looked at the group that was assembled around the island, which was everyone except Teddy, who had presumably located Bruce's meditation room and was on the path to finding himself once again. Everyone was wearing pretty much the same expression—poorly disguised worry, though on Ford it was closer to the surface, maybe because it was his house. Even though my dad and Sophie and I had been living there for the summer, it was his in a way that it wasn't ours.

"It's not great," Ford said, leaning closer to the phone. When Sophie had summoned us from the pool house, Ford had jumped into action, assessing the damage and realizing quickly he was out of his depth in terms of fixing things—which was when he called Rosie. He'd contacted my dad on the walkie, and he and Karen had made the trek from the guesthouse in the rain, so they were both there as well. But Hallie and I both seemed to be working hard, simultaneously, not to look at them. "So water's coming toward the house from the beach. It's not up to the house yet, but it looks like it might get here soon. And there's a leak in Bruce's office."

I heard Rosie draw in a worried breath, and I leaned forward, closer to the speakerphone. "It's not too bad, though," I said, not wanting to worry Rosie, who wouldn't be able to do anything about this from Los Angeles, where it almost never rained and they didn't have these kinds of problems. "Just a few inches of water, that's all. And we've got a bucket in there now, so . . ."

"You might need to get his memorabilia out of there," Rosie said, dropping her volume, and I had a feeling it was so Bruce wouldn't hear. I knew all too well that if Bruce heard that anything in his brag room was in danger, he'd be apoplectic, screaming at his poor interns to do something about it, even though they were all in Los Angeles and with no control over the weather. I also knew, when she said "memorabilia," what she really meant—Bruce's Spotlight award. It was his pride and joy, which was probably the reason Hallie had made sure it had been broken by Isabella and Olivia, the demon-twins who Hallie had sent here for the sole reason of wrecking Bruce's house. I'd smuggled the award out of the house and sent it to Ford, who'd gotten it fixed before bringing it back from Hawaii with him earlier this summer. So it was fixed but still precarious. And the thing was, the award wasn't really even Bruce's. It had been intended for Marcus Davidman, the acclaimed British documentarian. But the name had been read wrong at the ceremony and, apparently, the Brits who gave out the award had been too polite to correct the mistake—which meant Bruce's point of pride didn't even belong to him.

"What about the polar bear?" Rosie asked now, shaking me out of these thoughts. "That's not ruined, is it?" she asked hopefully.

"Afraid not," my dad said, leaning closer to the phone. "We've got candles and a flashlight and the windows boarded up in the pool house. Is there anything else we should be doing?"

"Yes," Rosie said, and I could hear the efficiency in her voice—it was why, when Ford had suggested calling her, I'd immediately felt more at ease. Rosie was endlessly competent and able to handle anything. I couldn't help thinking that if I'd just told her everything that had happened with Hallie as soon as I'd arrived in the Hamptons this summer, she could have told me exactly what to do and saved us all a lot of trouble. "You're going to need to put sandbags on the beach to keep the water away. If you don't, and the rain keeps up, there's a chance it could flood the house."

"Okay," Ford said, and I noticed he was starting to type a note on his phone. "They're where? In the garage?"

"Not in the garage," I said, leaning closer to the speaker. "I checked earlier."

"Well," Rosie said, her tone growing slightly annoyed—which was how you knew she was *really* annoyed—"They're normally there. But the garage is currently taken over by construction equipment because *someone* chained himself to a backhoe for the last two weeks and the construction crew couldn't do any work."

I shook my head then noticed that everyone else's reaction was pretty much the same—resigned disgust—except for Reid, who just looked perplexed. "Teddy," I said, by way of explanation, and he nodded.

"Anyway," Rosie said, "the sandbags are in the Van Allen house, down the street. They're storing them for us."

"Okay, we can get those," Ford said, typing on his phone.

"Also, is the power still on?" Rosie asked.

"Yes," my dad said, frowning slightly. "Why?"

"Just keep an eye on it," she said. "Call me if it goes off, okay?"

"Okay," my dad said, though I saw he was looking increasingly freaked out. "Anything else?"

"Just get the sandbags," Rosie said. "I'll call the Van Allens and let them know you're coming. And someone should probably check the basement. If water is starting to get in there, we've got big problems."

Rosie hung up then, and we all stared at each other for a moment, just trying to digest this. Then people sprang into action—my dad and Karen took Bruce's SUV to get the sandbags, and Reid and Josh headed to Bruce's office to move his memorabilia out of range of the leak, with instructions to do this as carefully as possible. Which left me, Hallie, Sophie, and Ford to go into the basement. There probably didn't need to be four of us doing this, but I would have felt weird sitting on the sidelines when there was a potential crisis brewing.

I realized, as I followed Ford down to the basement, Sophie

behind me and Hallie bringing up the rear, I'd never been in the basement before. There hadn't seemed to be much need, and if it really had been something awesome, Rosie would have shown it to me on the first tour of the house she'd given me, when I'd first arrived in the Hamptons.

And as Ford snapped on the lights on the wall and I looked around, I saw I hadn't been missing much. It was a long, rectangular space underneath the house, and it seemed mostly to be used for storage—but not in any kind of organized fashion. There were just boxes and piles of stuff spread around intermittently. I wasn't sure if Rosie was aware of the state of the basement or if it was one of the things on her to-do list she hadn't gotten to yet, because I couldn't imagine her knowing about it and letting it stay in this state.

"Oh," Sophie said, her voice disappointed, as she looked around once we'd all reached the bottom of the stairs. "I guess I just thought . . ."

"What?" Ford asked, raising an eyebrow at her.

"You know," Sophie said, gesturing vaguely toward the house above us. "Like, there would be a wine cellar or a fleet of vintage cars or a manservant or something down here."

"You know Bruce isn't James Bond or Tony Stark, right?" I asked her, and saw Sophie roll her eyes at me, her cheeks turning pink.

"Sorry," Ford said, and I could tell he was holding back a laugh. "Just junk we didn't really want to deal with, that's all. But I'll tell Bruce the James Bond thing. He'll *love* it."

There was a pause as we all looked around, and it became

clear that nobody really knew what to do next. "So," Hallie said, jumping in, "how do we tell if there's a leak?"

"I think we just have to check all the corners, make sure nothing's damp," Ford said, then shrugged. "I mean, I'm guessing. I've never had to deal with this before."

We all spread out, heading for the opposite corners of the space. I looked around as I headed for mine, seeing, mixed in with the boxes and out-of-style clothes, a huge set of encyclopedias, stretched out on a shelf that took up almost the length of the basement. "Hey," I said, and Ford looked over at me. I nodded at the encyclopedias. "Want me to look up how to check for leaks? You guys have, like, the entire alphabet."

Ford shook his head as he continued over to his corner. "Maybe if we didn't have the Internet," he said with a laugh. "Those were like the original Google."

I looked at the books for a moment longer and then headed to my corner. I felt around all the edges of the walls and ground, but it didn't seem like any water was coming in, and I felt myself let out a sigh of relief. Our house in Connecticut had flooded once a few years ago, and it had been horrible—me and my mom bailing buckets of water out while my stepfather, Walter, told us facts we didn't want to know about different freshwater fish. "I think we're okay over here," I said, straightening up. As I did, I lost my balance, wobbling in my bare feet, and reached out to steady myself.

Unfortunately, what I'd grabbed on to turned out to be a precarious pile of boxes that then toppled over, taking me down with it. "Ow," I muttered, pushing myself to my feet.

"You okay?" Ford called, and I glanced over to see he was looking at me, worried.

"I'm okay," I said, brushing some dust off my shirt and then giving him a thumbs-up I immediately regretted when he still looked concerned. He smiled and shook his head, then went back to his own corner. Now that I was on my feet again and done with my job, I started looking at what had pulled me down to the ground. It didn't take me long to realize this seemed to be the corner of Bruce's ex-wives' stuff. The boxes were labeled with names I recognized, but I had a feeling they'd been written by the current wife, since in addition to the names on the boxes— Ruby, Dakota, Peridot—there were lots of other comments I had a feeling hadn't been Bruce's doing.

I started stacking the boxes up again, wondering if we should probably just give this stuff to Goodwill, since I didn't think any of these women were coming back for it anytime soon. It was when I was stacking the last box that the bottom split open, sending a pile of stuff spilling out and landing at my feet. I sighed then started stacking it on top of Dakota's box. It wasn't until I'd piled the first few sweaters and pairs of shoes on top that I started to realize there was something odd about this stuff—or at least different than the other boxes. There seemed to be lots of books about flower arranging, for a start, and I found myself idly flipping through one, a little amazed that books like this existed.

A section toward the bottom of one of the pages caught my eye. I looked around quickly, but everyone else still seemed busy, which made me wonder if they were maybe doing a much more thorough job than I was, and then I turned back to the book.

Do not discount the "almost" flower. You find these in practically every bouquet . . . the flower that, for whatever reason, has not bloomed. I'm not referring to the young flowers that will open in a few days' time and add to the beauty of your arrangement. These are the flowers that might be open slightly but will never open more. Many arrangers discard these blooms, but I think they should never be cast aside. There is, after all, beauty in the almosts. In the potential.

"Gemma?"

My head snapped up from the book, and I saw Sophie standing in front of me, her head tilted to the side. "What's that?"

"It's . . . a book on flower arranging," I said, feeling my cheeks get hot as I said it. I shrugged and put it back on the pile as Ford and Hallie started to walk over as well. "I was just . . . um . . ."

"You don't have to be embarrassed," Sophie said, shooting me a grin. "We all know that's your secret passion."

"All okay?" Ford asked as he approched.

"Mine was dry," Sophie said.

Hallie nodded, joining us. "Mine too," she said.

"That's good," Ford said, letting out a sigh of relief. "We can always check again in a few hours, but hopefully we're in the clear." He looked at the boxes behind me. "Ah, you found the ex corner?"

"I did," I said, putting the last few items that had fallen out of the last box on top of the pile. I picked up the box that had fallen apart and started folding it up, seeing as I did the name that was written across the side. "But who's Bianca?"

"Oh," Ford said as he started to walk toward the stairs, the rest of us following behind him. "That's one of Bruce's exes."

I frowned. I thought I had known about all the women Bruce had been married to—even if I hadn't met them, I'd been on the other end of Ford's and Gwyneth's complaining about them. "Bianca?" I echoed, wondering how I could have missed this one.

"Yeah," Ford said as we all started to climb the stairs back up to the first floor. "She was a wannabe florist. They were only married, like, a month before they had it annulled so, according to Bruce, it doesn't really count. I think I only met her once, actually."

I stopped in my tracks, causing Sophie to bump into me. "Sorry," I said to her, starting to walk again. "But . . . what do you mean, annulled?"

"It's when a marriage is basically erased," Ford said as we all reached the top landing and he snapped off the lights, closing the door behind Hallie. "It's not a divorce; it's pretty much like you get a judge to declare it never really happened."

I shot Hallie a look, feeling my heart start to beat hard. Hallie looked back at me, and I could see she was thinking the same thing I was. This . . . *this* was what we needed to do. We had to make it like this marriage had never ever happened. And, apparently, there was a way to do that. "Oh," I said, when I realized Ford was still looking at me, waiting for me to reply. "That's . . . really interesting."

"Gemma," Ford said, looking at me closely, like he could tell what I was thinking. "What are you—"

But he didn't get any further with his question, because at that moment all the lights went off.

CHAPTER 8

I pressed the phone against my ear as I paced around the living room, willing Rosie to answer. My dad and Karen were still off getting the sandbags, and I was just praying the SUV was making it through. Most of what the news had been showing was stranded cars, the water coming up toward the side-view mirrors. But I needed to talk to someone who was calm and collected and could see the situation with perspective. And in the last few minutes, Ford had stopped being that person entirely.

"I can't get online," he said, his expression verging on panic as he looked between his phone and his laptop, then set both down and ran over to the console under the TV, the one I'd never even looked at before, and started fussing with the electronic devices underneath there. "There is no power going to the router. Which means"—he took a long, shaky breath, like he was trying to calm himself—"which means we have no Internet."

"The Wi-Fi's out?" I asked, and Ford nodded. "So just use your phone," I said with a shrug.

"I've tried," Ford said, still taking big breaths, like he was trying to stave off a panic attack. "But since there's no cell service, I'm not getting any Internet. We need Wi-Fi to get online, which we *really* don't have right now."

"Are you okay?" I asked just as the landline dropped the call again. I redialed Rosie's number. "I've never seen you like this."

"You've never seen me without Internet," Ford said, shooting me a wry smile. "It's not pretty."

"You don't have Internet when you're surfing," I pointed out, hoping maybe to drag him back to the land of the logical.

"I think," Ford said, taking another big breath, "it's more that we're in a crisis here." He went on, speaking fast. "Not the no-Internet crisis. But the storm. What if we need to figure something out, and we can't because there's *no Internet*?" His voice rose in volume on the last three words, and then he must have heard himself, because he shook his head. "I know I'm being crazy," he said a little ruefully. "I just don't think I'm going to be able to stop it."

"Well, try to calm down," I said before the call finally connected—going right to Rosie's voice mail. I left her a message that hopefully conveyed the situation with enough urgency that she would call me back as soon as possible. I set the phone down and looked around, feeling myself shiver. I didn't think it was my imagination—I was pretty sure it had just gotten a bit colder in the room.

The lights had come back on after a minute, but they were *definitely* not as bright as they'd been before, and they were flickering every few moments. But what was disturbing Ford the most, however, was that ever since the lights had gone out, we had no Internet connection. He wasn't getting any signal at all, even beyond Bruce's Wi-Fi, which I thought was probably due to the storm—in this weather, it seemed pretty likely that everyone was losing their cable connections.

"How can I calm down?" Ford muttered as he picked up his phone again, walking around with it, holding it up, like he was hoping against hope he might get a signal. "What are we supposed to *do* if we can't go online?"

"We'll handle it," I said, still trying to get used to this version of him—stressed out and worried and not thinking rationally. Which was actually a little bit of a relief, since he'd been seeing me that way a lot all summer. I looked up and saw Hallie standing in the doorway, motioning toward me. "Just . . . um . . . hang on." I walked over to her, still trying to get used to this. Only a few hours ago, if Hallie had motioned me toward her, I would have assumed it was because she had some diabolical plan in place for me.

"Hey," I said, and as I did, I realized how weird this was—just talking to Hallie this casually, no hidden messages or ulterior motives. "I mean, what?" I asked, making my voice much more unfriendly as I crossed my arms. "What do you want?"

"Annulment," Hallie said, her voice low, and I realized my hunch had been correct—she'd been thinking the same thing I had been when Ford had mentioned it.

I nodded. When Ford had first said it, it was like a get-out-of-jail-free card had appeared—like maybe we could get this terrible mistake over and done with, and *fast*.

"If we can get them to break up," she said, eyes darting over my shoulder for just a second, like she was worried our parents were going to walk in and hear this, "there wouldn't be a long, drawn-out divorce. They would just both realize they made a mistake, and it would be like it never happened."

I nodded, thinking just how good that sounded. I hadn't wanted to let myself, but whenever I'd imagined a life that would involve Karen and her kids—the people I'd be forced to see on a regular basis—it had made me almost as panicky as Ford without the Internet. "Yes," I said firmly, feeling like this was the first thing we'd had to some sort of plan. "Let's do it."

"Okay," Hallie said, pulling out her phone. "So I'll see what's involved with an annulment, and you—"

I shook my head, feeling my stomach plunge with disappointment, wondering why this had to be happening *now*. "The Internet's out," I said, realizing I wasn't sure when we'd be able to get more information on this. "I'm not sure for how long."

"Oh," Hallie said, lowering her phone. She bit her lip, and I could see she was almost as thrown by this as Ford had been. "Okay. Well . . ."

The phone in my hand started ringing, and I saw it was Rosie. "Have to take this," I said, and Hallie nodded. After a moment's thought, I answered it on the way to the kitchen, worried that if I answered it when Ford was in earshot, he'd spend the whole time yelling to Rosie about how tragic this was, and trying to get her to somehow fix this situation—from California. "Hey, Rosie," I said as I walked into the kitchen, where Sophie was sitting at the kitchen counter.

She jumped up when she saw me. "I have to talk to you," she said.

I nodded at her and then pointed to my phone. "Can you hear me?" I asked.

"Yes," Rosie said, though I noticed with alarm that she was a lot more static-y than she'd been before, her voice cutting out every few seconds. "What's going on?"

"So, the lights went out again," I said, crossing my fingers that Rosie would have some way to fix this and could restore the Internet before Ford lost his mind. "They came back on again, though. But—"

"But not as bright, right?" Rosie asked, her voice worried. "And flickering a little?"

"Yeah," I said, looking around at the light above the kitchen counter, the one that was cutting out every few seconds before returning again. "How'd you know that?"

"The power went out," Rosie said with a sigh. I looked around at all the lights that were still on, at the microwave clock flashing REPROGRAM.

"I don't think it did," I said. "We still have lights and power. We just don't have the Internet," I added quickly, knowing Ford would have wanted me to have led with this information, probably before even saying hello.

"No, the power's definitely out," Rosie said again, her voice grim. "The lights and power that are on right now are coming from the generator."

"Oh," I said, feeling myself breathe a little easier. "So then we're fine. The generator will keep the lights on."

"For a while," she said. "It's only got so much fuel. I'm going to need you to make sure the propane tanks are full, okay, Gemma? Otherwise the generator's going to stop working, and then you *really* will have no power."

"Okay," I said, nodding as I looked around for someone else who could handle this for me. But my dad was gone, Rosie was thousands of miles away, and Ford was currently focused only on getting his Internet connection back. Realizing it was up to me to take care of this, I grabbed a piece of paper from the kitchen counter and started writing down her instructions—where the propane tanks could be found, how often I needed to fill them—as Sophie looked on, her eyes widening as the instruction list got longer and longer.

"Got it?" Rosie asked as I set my pen down.

"I think so," I said, looking at the scrawl of notes that covered the paper. "But what are we going to do about the Internet?"

"Ford's freaking out, huh?" Rosie asked, and I thought back to my conversation with Hallie—how we really needed the Internet as well if we were going to figure this out.

"Right," I said quickly. "Ford. Totally just Ford."

"For whatever reason, the cable wasn't hooked up to the generator," she said with a sigh. "I've been on Bruce to fix it for a while, but—"

"So no Internet until the real power comes back on?" I asked, hearing the shock in my voice when I spoke. Sophie, across the counter from me, was looking equally alarmed.

"I'm afraid not," Rosie said. "So just—wait, hold on. Bruce!"

she said, just before I heard sounds of a scuffle, like the phone was being dropped.

"Gemma!" It was Bruce on the other end of the phone, his voice loud and excited. "Quite a storm you guys are having out there, huh?" Without giving me time to respond, he was going on. "Listen, I need you to be my eyes and ears out there, okay? I was thinking about doing a disaster movie, and I need you to soak up details for research. And make sure your dad's paying attention, okay? You don't get opportunities like this every day."

"Sure," I said, having learned from years of experience with Bruce that it was usually best to just agree with him and hope he would forget about it and move on to something else by the next time you spoke. "Um . . . did you want to hear about the house?" I asked. If I owned a beachfront mansion that currently had a hurricane bearing down on it, I would imagine I'd be slightly concerned about it.

"I'm sure you're handling it," Bruce said, his voice now cutting out at almost every other word. "And don't forget—notes! I'm looking for a new project, and this could be—" But then the static took over his voice entirely, and a second later I saw the call had been dropped—even the landline reception was getting dangerously close to disappearing altogether.

"Everything okay?" Sophie asked, frowning as she looked at me.

"Well . . ." I said, looking down at the list of Rosie's notes and then folding the paper and sticking it in the pocket of my hoodie. "I hope so. We don't have any Internet, but we should be able to keep the power on for a while longer, at least."

Sophie nodded. "Oh, that's good," she said vaguely, then leaned forward across the counter toward me. "I *have* to talk to you," she said. But before I could even ask what about, she was continuing on. "It's about Reid." I felt myself smile. Sophie's tone was the one she normally reserved for crushes and boyfriends. It seemed my hunch that her feelings had changed was right on.

"I don't know," she said with a sigh. "I just can't stop thinking about him. I think it started on the boat. You know my thing for guys in formal wear."

"I do," I said, trying to suppress a shudder, flashing back to the prom, when Sophie had pretty much been crushing on every guy in her immediate vicinity—something her date hadn't been too happy about, to say the least.

"But I don't know! I mean, we're all here . . . stuck in this house together . . . and he just keeps on looking cuter."

"Wow," I said, giving her a smile. "You really *do* like him." It was throwing me for a little bit of a loop, simply because Sophie had always, for as long as I'd known her, gone for bad boys. Only just last week I'd been trying to convince her that maybe she should think about a good guy for once, and she had basically brushed this aside.

"What do you think?" she asked, biting her bottom lip nervously.

"I think it's great," I said immediately. Reid could drive me crazy sometimes, but he *was* a good guy. You could see that almost as soon as you met him. "I think you should tell him how you feel."

Sophie let out a long, shaky breath, but I could see she was thinking about it. "This is funny," she said after a moment, gesturing between the two of us.

"What is?" I asked.

"I was, like, *just* telling you the same thing about Ford," she said. "When I told you to tell him how you felt? I guess I should have been listening to my own advice." She looked at me closely. "So, did you do it? What's going on there?"

"I don't know," I said. I glanced behind me, outside where the wind was still throwing the trees around and there was what looked like a small lake on the deck as the pool started to overflow. Should I be talking to my best friend about boys while there was a natural disaster happening a few feet away? But after watching, worried, for a moment I figured there was nothing I could really do to prevent it until we got the sandbags. There wasn't anything we could do about the Internet, and I wasn't exactly looking forward to being the one to tell Ford that. And I would absolutely go and replace the fuel in the generator—but I didn't have to do it right this second, I reasoned. And it felt like so much had happened, and I hadn't been able to discuss any of it with Sophie, which was just unacceptable. So I settled down onto the stool by the kitchen counter, and Sophie sat on the one across from me. I was more than ready to have a talk, a real one, with my best friend.

"So, we were in the pool house before . . ." I leaned forward and started to tell Sophie what had happened—or hadn't happened—when we'd been standing close, holding our pinkie swear for much longer than necessary. I told her about how I lost my nerve, and how I was worried about things changing between us if I told him how I was feeling. Then Sophie needed to fill me in on just what happened with Reid and the boat, which led to a discussion of the fight Hallie and I had that essentially stopped the party—even though the storm would no doubt have done it a few minutes later anyway.

I was telling her about my dad's revelation that he was suddenly *married*—Sophie had grabbed my arm when I'd told her—and had just said that Hallie and I were planning on working together to break them up. I expected Sophie to have an opinion immediately, to jump in with her take on things. But when I'd finished talking, she just leaned back against her seat, her expression thoughtful.

"What?" I finally asked as her silence stretched on and I felt I couldn't take it any longer.

"I don't know," she said. "I'm not sure if it's the best idea."

"Working with Hallie?" I asked, and nodded. "I know, Ford said the same thing. But—"

"Not working with Hallie," Sophie clarified. "I meant trying to break up your dad and Karen."

I blinked at her. I had expected Sophie, who'd been with me through this whole thing, to be on my side. "You understand why I have to do this, right?" I asked, hearing the incredulity in my tone. "I mean, I'm just supposed to let this happen? I'm supposed to let myself be related to Hallie—possibly for life?"

Sophie shrugged. "I just think . . . I mean, your dad's been alone for a long time now. Your mom has Walter. . . ." I made a face, but Sophie continued on. "And the fact that he picked Karen again, after all these years . . . maybe there's really something there. Maybe your dad gets to be happy for once."

I just stared at her. "You don't understand," I finally said, shaking my head. There were some things you couldn't know until you'd been through them, I figured. And Sophie's parents were still together, running their joint therapy practice and taking power walks on the weekends. She didn't know what this was like. A moment later, though, I realized Ford *did*. And he'd still had almost the same reaction as Sophie. But I pushed this away as just a coincidence, nothing more than that.

"Just think about it, okay?" Sophie asked. I nodded, even though I knew I wasn't going to change my mind.

"Hello?" a confused-sounding voice called from the hallway. Sophie and I glanced at each other. "Hi?" I called back.

"I think that sounded like Reid," Sophie said, standing up. Sure enough, a moment later Reid appeared in the kitchen, relief washing over his face when he saw me and Sophie.

"Oh wow, I'm so happy to see you guys," he said. "This house is *really* big. And really confusing."

"Did you get lost?" Sophie asked sympathetically, but I could tell we were only a few seconds away from hearing her flirting voice. She really *did* like him. "Poor Reid."

Reid took the seat next to Sophie at the kitchen counter. "Every time I thought I had my bearings, I'd turn down the wrong hallway. And then I got turned around in the wing over that way," he said, gesturing. "I kept looking for my room and not finding it."

"But nobody's staying there," I said, feeling myself frown. I was pretty sure Karen had put everyone a little closer to the center of the house and not in the rooms Bruce reserved for executives he didn't like very much. "Wasn't that your first clue? That all the rooms were empty?"

"Not all of them," Reid said. "There was one where the light was on—and I was pretty sure I heard someone . . . or maybe it was the TV. . . ."

I felt myself frown. Nobody was staying in that part of the house—I was sure of it. I figured maybe when the generator kicked on, it had turned on some lights or a TV where it shouldn't have. I made a mental note to check it out later—after I'd refilled the generator's fuel. Of course. A moment later, though, I realized what it was. "Teddy's off on a vision quest or something," I said, dismissing this. "You probably heard him."

Reid nodded, still looking unsure. "I guess so."

"Well, you're here now," Sophie said, sliding her stool even closer to Reid's, her flirty voice now present and accounted for. "I'm so glad."

"Yeah?" Reid asked, his voice shooting up about an octave, his cheeks turning bright red.

"Yeah," Sophie practically purred, which I took as my cue to leave.

"Okay, I'll see you guys," I said, hurriedly getting up and heading for the door.

"No, no, stay," Sophie said, even though her tone told me she meant exactly the opposite of this.

I headed out of the kitchen and paused in the hallway, not sure exactly where to go. I didn't even want to see Ford, which was really unusual for me. But I knew he would ask me about the Internet, and I wasn't sure I was up to handling his reaction.

I passed the living room and saw that the room was now empty and the TV was off—Ford must have gone to mourn the lack of Internet elsewhere. There was only one light on in the room, but I wasn't sure if it just hadn't been turned off, or if this was another generator thing. But either way, the dark, quiet room looked like just the kind of peaceful place I needed to gather my thoughts at the moment. I flopped down on one of the leather couches, leaning back against it and closing my eyes for a moment. I was feeling just how long the day had been so far, and how confusing. I was feeling myself start to breathe a little easier when I heard a voice say, "Gemma?"

My eyes flew open, and I looked over to see Josh sitting on the couch opposite mine. "Hey," I said, sitting up straighter, squinting as my eyes adjusted to him in the darkness. He was wearing a sweat shirt with a mournful-looking turtle across the front, which I recognized as the star of the animated time-travel movie *Time Crawls*. I figured in the clothes emergency, it must have come from Bruce's swag pile. "Nice sweat shirt."

"Thanks," he said, glancing down at it. "I think it suits me." He gave me a slightly embarrassed smile. "Sorry if I scared you."

"No, it's okay," I said, now that my heart rate was returning to something like normal again. "I just came in here to try to get some peace and quiet."

"Me too," he said, and I felt myself laugh. "There's just . . . a lot going on here."

"Yeah," I said, realizing his side of this for the first time. Probably the last place he wanted to be was stuck in his current girlfriend's house, with his mother and sister, his sister's boyfriend, and the girl who he'd liked at one point. None of us really wanted to be here together, but Josh probably had the most legitimate reasons for that. "I'm sorry about Gwyneth," I said quietly. If *I* felt betrayed by what she'd done with the footage, I could only imagine how Josh might feel.

He nodded and then looked down at his hands. "I mean, it's not like it was really that serious," he said. "Not like—" He stopped talking midsentence and looked up at me. When he didn't finish speaking, I realized what he meant, and I felt my cheeks start to warm up. He'd meant *not like me.*

I was trying not to, but I suddenly flashed back to the two of us in the freezer, standing close, just for a second, a heartbeat away from kissing. And the news I'd gotten days later, that the day after our freezer encounter he'd come by the house looking for me—only to meet Gwyneth. We'd never talked about what had happened—or had almost happened—between us. I took a breath to speak, but then I just let it out, not even sure what I wanted to say. Because what did that mean about Ford? About what was happening with my dad and Karen?

"It's funny," Josh said, and I looked over at him. "Well, not *funny*, exactly," he amended a moment later. "I just . . . I realized I'm not mad at you anymore."

"You're not?" I asked, and I could hear the hope in my voice as I said it. It was what I'd thought when we were in the freezer together—that it seemed like he was on the road to forgiving me but he hadn't been 100 percent sure.

Josh shook his head. "I'm not," he said. "I think I got over it a while back, but I hadn't realized it until this stuff with Gwyneth. It just made things clear."

"It did?" I asked, trying and failing to find a connection between the two.

"Yeah," he said, nodding. "It hit me that she was doing something that was going to hurt Hallie and hurt my family, and she just didn't care. And I realized you'd actually been trying to make things right. You may not have gone about it in the best way. . . ." I smiled at that, even as I could feel myself blush. "But it was coming from a good place. I finally saw that."

I nodded, just taking this all in. It felt like a weight had been lifted off my shoulders, one that had been pressing down on them for so long, it was like I'd stopped noticing it was there. "Well . . . I'm glad," I finally said, giving him a small smile. "I really was . . . I mean, I just wanted to try to make things right."

"I know that now," Josh said, his voice quiet.

I looked over at him, and he gave me a small smile. I gave him one back, and I noticed things between us didn't feel quite so charged any longer. It just felt peaceful, like we'd both said what we needed to.

"Sorry to interrupt," a voice behind us said. I turned around, already knowing what I would see, my stomach sinking. It was

Ford, looking between me and Josh, his expression confused and a little bit hurt.

"You weren't," I said, jumping up immediately, thinking that in the wake of telling Ford that Josh and I had some history, the last thing he'd needed to see was the two of us, sitting across from each other in the dark. *If* Ford even liked me, and if he did, if he wanted anything to happen between us, which was something I still wasn't entirely sure about.

"Just wanted to let you know your dad and Karen are back with the sandbags," Ford said.

I felt myself breathe out. "They made it back?"

"Yeah," Ford said, "although Paul said they wouldn't have if it hadn't been next door. And even then—he's afraid water got into the engine, so he said he didn't want to drive the car again until it gets checked out."

I nodded, trying to look like this wasn't scaring me—that the weather was bad enough that even going *next door* had maybe wrecked Bruce's giant, military-grade SUV. "But they got the sandbags?"

Ford nodded. "And a lot of pizza. So dinner's happening in the kitchen."

"Pizza?" Josh asked, sounding confused. I didn't blame him—how had they managed that if they could barely make it next door?

"Apparently, the Van Allens had ordered some, and when the pizza guy made it to their house, he gave them all the pies he had with him. He'd decided it was going to be his last delivery of the night."

"Great," I said. Ford looked between me and Josh again, then started to walk toward the kitchen. I followed behind him, not wanting him to get the wrong impression or think there was anything going on between us. I put my hands in the front pocket of my hoodie, and as I did, I felt Rosie's list of instructions that was folded up there. I hesitated but then continued walking toward the kitchen, my stomach already growling at the freshly baked pizza smell. I would check on the generator after dinner. It would be fine until then. And then, thinking only about the dinner I was suddenly famished for, I continued on into the kitchen.

CHAPTER 9

I turned over on my side, looking out my window, at the rain streaking down the windowpane, and the rattling of the glass from the wind. The occasional flash of lightning cut across the sky, throwing everything into brightness for just a second before disappearing again. I pushed aside the candles and matches on my bedside table—since we only had one flashlight, it was living downstairs for the moment—and picked up my phone and looked at the time. I'd been in bed for hours, lying awake, and it was still only twelve thirty. Everyone had gone to bed (carrying our just-in-case-of-blackout supplies) almost immediately after dinner, which was sure to go down in history as one of the most awkward meals ever.

There was the fact that, as we sat around the kitchen table, choosing from any of the four pies we had available to us (sadly, none of them were pineapple, pepperoni, and sausage, but I'd known from the outset that would have been too much to hope for), it was becoming clearer to everyone that nobody was leaving the house tonight.

According to what my dad and Karen had heard on the radio, the storm was now classified as a hurricane, which meant there wasn't any hope for roads to open up, at least not in the immediate future. So the revelation that everyone was going to be spending the night didn't help give a great start to the dinner. I spent the whole time barely able to look at my dad and Karen, but also not wanting them to suspect anything, so I pretended I was way too interested in what the person next to me had to say—unfortunately for me, I was sitting next to Reid. And then there was the matter of the vibe between Hallie and Teddy, which was *really* strained and getting worse by the minute. Teddy had emerged from his "walkabout," drawn by the scent of the pizza (that he then didn't eat, because it wasn't vegan) but it was clear theirs was not going to be an amicable breakup. You could cut the tension between them with a knife, and the ever-increasing volume of the rain and thunder really didn't help any. Everyone had scattered pretty much immediately after dinner, each person to their own rooms—or the guesthouse, in the case of my dad and Karen.

I'd been having trouble falling asleep, which at first I figured was because I didn't usually go to bed at ten o'clock at night. But as it got later, and I was still lying there, I realized it was my thoughts—not the time—that were keeping me awake.

They were swirling—my feelings for Ford, whatever was happening with me and Josh, and Hallie, if I could actually trust her, if we could pull this off. And then there was the fact that both Sophie and Ford had basically told me to back off my plan to break up my dad and Karen. I tried to reason this away, telling myself it was just because they weren't in my shoes, that they didn't understand. And I was really almost starting to believe it.

And there was also the feeling I was forgetting something. It kept needling at me, hovering around the edges of my consciousness, but never coming forward enough to actually let me know what it might be. It was like the feeling I sometimes had when I left the house and it started raining—that *Have I closed my bedroom window?* feeling—nudging me every now and then.

I rolled onto my back and stared up at the ceiling, listening to the sound of the rain outside my window. This wasn't the nice, calm pitter-patter of rain that made things seem nice and cozy—this was rain that was driving and angry and clearly not letting up anytime soon.

Trying to put Sophie's and Ford's words—and their expressions—out of my head, I started thinking about the annulment idea again. It really did seem like the ideal solution. And despite what Sophie and Ford were saying, it didn't mean my dad wasn't getting to be happy. If this marriage were to crash and burn in a few years, wouldn't that be worse than nipping it in the bud from the beginning? Wasn't I actually *saving* him from some pain and heartbreak? I instinctively reached for my phone but then remembered the lack of Internet a few seconds later. The problem with this was that neither Hallie nor I had any idea what an annulment involved, and what the qualifications for it were. I probably could have pressed Ford for more details, but since he was already against this plan, I wasn't sure he'd give very many details to me. If only there was some other non-Internet way of finding out information, especially when going to a library was totally out of the question. Some way I could find out information without having to ask anyone . . .

I sat up with a jolt, remembering what I'd seen in the basement—the "original Google," as Ford had dubbed it.

The encyclopedias.

I got up, pulling my hoodie more tightly around me, and then hurried down the hallway. Even though I had a number of explanations lined up if anyone needed them—I needed a glass of water/wanted to check on the state of the storm/missed the polar bear—I still felt like I was about to get found out. I looked around once before crossing to the staircase, and then standing at the edge of it, where the stairs met the wall, since Ford had told me that stairs don't squeak there (I hadn't wanted to know how he knew that).

"Hey!" It was barely more than a whisper, but I jumped and whirled around, my heart pounding. Hallie was standing in front of me, a sweat shirt over her pajamas, her arms crossed.

"Jeez," I muttered, pressing my hand over my heart, which was racing. "What are you doing?"

"What are *you* doing?" she shot back.

"I'm . . ." I started to run though my list of excuses but then dismissed them one by one. "Why are you up?" I asked, rather than answer her question.

"I couldn't sleep," she said. "And then I heard someone sneaking around—"

"How can you *hear* someone sneaking around?" I asked, rolling my eyes. "It's not like that's a sound."

"And yet here we are," she said in a tone of faux amazement.

"Listen," I said, taking a step closer—and then immediately taking one back. Hallie's eyes were puffy and red, and her face was blotchy—like she'd just had an extended crying jag. "Whoa," I said, then realized that probably had not been the politest response to her appearance. "I mean . . . you okay?"

"I'm fine," she snapped. "And I'll be better when you tell me what you're doing."

"Fine," I shot back at her, realizing a moment too late I should tell her this stuff—we were supposed to be working together. But the impulse to keep things from Hallie, and protect my secrets, was pretty deeply ingrained. "I had an idea. About the annulment thing. We could research it in the encyclopedias. The ones in the basement?"

Hallie raised an eyebrow at me. "Not a bad idea," she conceded. "You're going there now?" I nodded. "Then I'm coming."

"I can do it on my own," I said, even though a piece of me was secretly glad. I wasn't a huge fan of basements, even when there wasn't a storm raging outside.

"Yeah," Hallie said, shaking her head. "Not going to happen. Lead on."

We walked down the steps together, and as I glanced over

at her, I couldn't help but smile. Even though I was sure Hallie wasn't happy to look the way she did, seeing her like this—in pajamas that were giveaway promo items for Bruce's last movie, her hair sticking up funny in the back—made me think I was seeing the girl I used to know, not the one I'd met again this summer, the one who dressed like she'd just stepped out of a J.Crew catalog, perfectly done and coiffed. But, instead, the tomboy I'd known when we were eleven, the one who'd been my friend.

We were halfway to the basement door when I heard a rattling sound coming from the kitchen—like someone was moving around the pots and pans. I froze and then saw Hallie had stopped too, her eyes wide.

"What is that?" she whispered to me.

"I don't know," I whispered back. "Maybe someone getting a snack?" But even as I said it, I didn't really believe it. First of all, no lights were on in the kitchen. And it was late—did I really believe someone was going to go downstairs and heat up some food? Without bothering to turn on any lights? "Hello?" I called in the direction of the kitchen, but there was nothing but silence.

"Maybe it's a ghost," Hallie said, clearly trying to lighten the mood. "Or," she continued, her voice growing more serious, "a mouse?"

I felt myself shudder, and I had a very strong urge to jump onto the nearest high surface. I honestly might have preferred to deal with a ghost. "You think?" I asked, my voice coming out high-pitched and squeaky.

"Oh right," Hallie said, rolling her eyes, "I'd forgotten you hate mice."

"Who *likes* mice?" I pointed out.

"Well, cats, snakes, Cinderella . . ." Hallie said, listing them off on her fingers.

"Stop it," I said. Even though I had a feeling she was trying to make a joke of the situation, I couldn't help suppressing a shudder. We continued on toward the basement door, but before I opened it, I glanced back to the kitchen for just a moment. I tried to tell myself it had been nothing, just pans that had been stacked precariously shifting around, or something. But I couldn't shake the feeling that it had been something else. This nagged at me until I had a thought.

"I think it was Teddy," I said as I pulled open the basement door and turned the light on, and Hallie and I walked down the stairs together. He'd made such a big show about turning down the pizza at dinner, but I'd been able to tell that he was hungry.

"Then why weren't the lights on?"

"When he's eating something he feels ethically compromised eating—like dairy or, you know, anything that tastes good—he never likes to admit it. So he was probably just getting a snack in the dark." We reached the bottom of the steps, and Hallie stopped.

"Wow," she said from the bottom step as she looked around. "It's different at night."

"Yeah," I agreed, pulling my hoodie around me again. Even though all the lights were on, the basement was somehow much spookier now than it had been just a few hours ago. The shadows seemed to be stretching longer, and there seemed to be more hidden dark corners. And even though I knew the object in the far corner was just a dress left over from when Bruce's ex-wife Ruby wanted to be a fashion designer, I couldn't stop feeling like it was going to come to life at any moment. "Let's just get the encyclopedia and get out of here."

"Agreed," Hallie said, looking around with a little shiver.

We found some old suitcases and stacked them together so I could stand on them and reach the shelf where the encyclopedias were. "Jeez," I said as I climbed up and looked at them, trying not to cough. "I don't think anyone's used these in a *long* time." There was a thick layer of dust lying across them, and I tried to make myself breathe through my nose as I looked for the *A* volume—they also didn't seem to be alphabetized, which was making my job harder at the moment. "Hold on a sec," I said, idly wondering what the logic was that had put *B* next to *Q*, which was next to *K*. It took a minute, but I finally spotted *A* next to *X*. I pulled down the *A* volume and stepped off the suitcase. "Want to look at this upstairs?" I asked, and Hallie nodded immediately.

"So," she asked, when we were almost to the top of the staircase, "what's going on with you and Ford?" I looked over at her sharply, and she gave me a faint smile. "You guys have a whole vibe going on," she said. "And he kept looking at you during dinner."

"Really?" I asked, wondering how I'd failed to pick up on that. "I mean, it's none of your business."

There was a long pause, and then Hallie shrugged. "You're right," she said. "I guess . . . I mean, we were pretending to be friends earlier this summer. I forget sometimes it wasn't real."

I swallowed hard, looking down at the ground. I wanted to agree with her, since this was the same way I felt. But what if this was just another trick? Get me to be vulnerable, admit to something she would just use against me later. "Yeah," I finally said. Even if it was a trick, this was the truth.

We headed up from the basement after that, and when I passed the kitchen—even though it probably had just been Teddy—I paused, waiting to hear the worst.

I listened as hard as I could, but there was only silence, so after a moment I flipped on the light switch, dreading seeing something horrible and furry scurrying across the countertop. But there was nothing except the kitchen we'd left after dinner, no other sounds or movement, so I let out a breath I hadn't realized I'd been holding as we passed the kitchen and went into the living room.

After making sure nobody was there, we sat on the couch that faced the door so that nobody would be able to sneak up on us. And even though we were reading through the encyclopedia together, we were sitting on opposite ends of the couch, the book on the center cushion between us—just in case anyone else walked by, it wouldn't look like we were teaming up together at all.

"Okay," I said, as I flipped the pages, feeling myself frown. I was getting a little worried as I caught some of the images—this looked *really* out of date. There was a picture of someone standing next to a "computer" that was big enough to take over a whole room. "Think this is still good?" I asked as I turned the book toward her more so she could see just how dated this looked. "I mean . . . a lot of this information seems to be from last century."

"I'm sure it's fine," Hallie said, but I could hear the doubt in her voice as she looked at the pictures as I flipped through them. "What does it say?"

"Okay," I said, my eyes scanning down the page. There was a lot of legal terminology, and I really didn't understand half of what I was reading. "There needs to be cause," I said, looking up at her. "Like fraud or irreconcilable differences."

"All right," Hallie said, nodding.

"It also says there's a time limit on when you can get a marriage annulled," I said, leaning closer to the book and trying not to sneeze.

"Well, how long?" Hallie said, leaning over my shoulder to read as well.

"It doesn't say," I said, going back to the top and reading the entry again in case I had missed something. But I hadn't—it just wasn't there. No wonder nobody used these stupid things anymore.

"What do you think that means?" Hallie asked, looking at me and twisting her hands together. "Like, a week? A month?"

"I don't know," I said, looking back down at the page, like it was magically going to produce some new information for me. "But it sounds like we should really do this as soon as possible, just to be on the safe side. Right?"

Hallie nodded. She pulled the book closer to her, and I saw her read the entry once over again before she shut the book. "Right," she agreed. "And we might not get a better situation than this. We're all trapped here, after all. In a stressful situation. We might be able to do this."

"So we'll start tomorrow," I said, and Hallie nodded.

"Tomorrow," she agreed. She leaned across the table toward me, lowering her voice, even though I was sure we were the only ones still awake. "So, what did you have in mind?"

CHAPTER 10

"**W**hat do you think?" Hallie asked, looking away from the wall of monitors and over to me. "Are we ready to do this?"

I took a deep breath and glanced at the monitor on the lower right-hand side. It was the next morning, and we were in the security center of the house—yet another room of Bruce's I'd never been into, and one I only knew about because of something Ford had once mentioned in passing to me. Apparently, Bruce had gone crazy with security a few years ago, when one of his prized pieces of movie memorabilia had disappeared during a party. The whole house had been set up by all these professional security consultants, who, I had no doubt, had charged Bruce an arm and a leg. But according to Ford, as soon as the system was installed, Bruce lost interest, especially when nothing else of his had ever been stolen again.

So while there were motion detectors and cameras set up, for the most part they were deactivated, and this room—a small room off the garage I'd never even paid any attention to before—went unused. Until today.

The room was small, and really built for one person, but Hallie and I had squeezed in, bringing an extra chair with us. A curved desk with a rolling chair faced a wall of TV screens—presumably, this was where the security guard who Bruce had never hired would have sat and made sure everything was on the up and up.

It had taken us a little bit of time to get everything set up again, but once we figured it out, it had been simple enough. And now we were looking at all the main rooms of the house, as well as the front driveway, pool, and areas around the property. (None of the bedrooms had been equipped with cameras, I had been very relieved to learn. And I also couldn't help being very glad that Gwyneth hadn't seemed aware of this technology when she was filming her documentary—it had been bad enough to know everyone had been walking around the house with a camera clipped to them for a while there, without also being filmed by security cameras without our knowledge.)

Hallie and I had stayed up most of the night, trading ideas and making plans, and out of the corner of my eye, I saw her hide a yawn behind her hand. It had taken us a while to hit on something we both thought was feasible and could work (Hallie had been a big fan of seeing how effective hypnosis could be, but I'd shot that down until she'd finally given up on it). The one conclusion we'd both come to was that if we were going to split up our parents, they had to think it was *their* idea. They both had to believe they had these irreconcilable differences—which they *did*, of course; it was just that neither of them could see it right now.

I looked at the monitors, all of them still turned off, reflecting me and Hallie looking at ourselves. I took a deep breath and then nodded. "Let's do it," I said. We'd both felt weird about turning these on before we needed them because essentially we'd be spying on the group. But this really was the last minute—if we didn't move soon, the breakfast that had taken us two tries and an hour to prepare was going to go cold.

Hallie flipped the switch, there was a little static, and then, one by one, each monitor came to life, showing a different part of the house. We hadn't been able to figure out how to turn only one on, so I was trying not to look at the other ones, just at the ones at the lower left—the ones that showed the outside, kitchen, and living room of the guesthouse. I saw Karen pass into frame as she walked into the kitchen, yawning, opening and closing cabinet doors, clearly looking for something.

"I told you," Hallie said, smiling faintly as she watched her mother on-screen.

"Jeez," I said, shaking my head. Hearing about Karen's coffee addiction—one of the cornerstones of our plan—had me rethinking my devotion to my morning latte. Clearly, it was a slippery slope.

"Yep," Hallie said, still not taking her eyes from the screen. "She once had a full-on meltdown when we were on a plane and they only had decaf."

I started to reply when there was a flash of movement on one of the upper monitors, and I felt my eyes dart up to it instinctively. The upper monitors showed the east wing hallway and the kitchen. The kitchen was empty—but had someone just been passing through, too fast for me to get a real look at? But if that were the case, why were the lights still off? But a second later Teddy wandered into view in the east wing hallway monitor, and he sank down to the ground in lotus pose. Clearly, his walkabout was still going on.

Realizing I must have just seen Teddy—walking about—I focused back on the guesthouse. Karen's search was getting increasingly agitated, and next to me, I saw Hallie smile. "Okay," she said, giving me a nod. "Let's do this." I grabbed the covered tray that was resting next to me on the small desk, Hallie pushed open the door, and we both stepped outside.

The rain had been beating down all night, and we'd both gotten drenched on our walk from the kitchen out here. The ground was soaked, and muddy, and I hadn't taken more than two steps before I felt my feet slide out from under me.

"You okay?" Hallie was gripping my elbow, steadying me, and after finding my footing again, I nodded.

"Yeah," I said, raising my voice to be heard over the wind, which was blowing harder than ever. For just a second I looked out to the ocean, which was churned up, the waves bigger than I'd ever seen them. The thought of Ford out there, surfing in that . . . I felt myself shiver, and was beyond glad I'd spoken to him when I did. What if he hadn't just happened to mention he was planning going surfing in what was essentially a deathtrap? I knew now, though, that I no longer had to worry about it. Ford had made me a promise, and he'd never broken one of those to me, not as long as we'd known each other. "Let's go!" I yelled to Hallie, and we started moving again, both of us more cautiously than before, despite the fact that we were now utterly soaked through, and we'd only been outside for a few seconds.

By the time we reached the guesthouse door, I wasn't sure I'd ever been so drenched in my entire life. I felt like I could have wrung out my hair into a pretty substantial puddle, and my clothes were so sodden that they were starting to get heavy, stretching down with the weight of the water.

"Ugh," Hallie said as we huddled under the guesthouse's tiny overhang that mostly seemed to be decorative, since I was still getting really wet.

"I know," I said, brushing my hand across my face and then shaking off the droplets. Hallie knocked on the door, loudly, and we looked at each other, both of us smiling brightly and facing the door.

It opened a second later, and a confused—and slightly grumpy-looking—Karen was standing behind it. "What are you girls doing?" she asked, her voice going up on the last word. She pulled Hallie inside, out of the rain, and motioned for me to follow. She shut the door behind her, and I breathed out, grateful to be dry and feeling warmer immediately. "Why are you running around in this?" Karen asked, looking from me to Hallie.

"Well . . ." Hallie started as I took a step toward the kitchen and set down the tray—it had started to get *really* heavy.

"Kare-bear?" my dad called, and Hallie and I exchanged a

look of horror. But *what*? I tried not to let my face reflect what I was feeling. I'd never had to hear my dad call my mother any cutesy nicknames, and I really preferred things to stay that way. "Is someone here?"

My dad rounded the corner, his jaw falling open in surprise as he saw me and Hallie standing together, but then he re-grouped a moment later. "Hi, girls," he said, and I could hear the wariness in his voice, and I saw the look he threw Karen, trying to see if she knew what this was about.

"So we decided to bury the hatchet," Hallie said, just like we'd planned. "From here on out, no more fighting on boats and bringing shame to sea captains. We're going to get along."

Karen and my dad exchanged a longer look this time— surprise mixed with something else—something closer to hope. "Just like that?" she asked, looking between the two of us.

"We had some time to talk about it last night," I said, going into my part of the script we'd worked out. "And we decided there was no point in not getting along."

"Well," my dad said, his eyebrows flying up. "That's . . . Well, it's surprising, girls, given what happened at Hallie's party."

Hallie and I exchanged a glance. I had been hoping my father would just accept this and move on, but the era of my dad barely paying attention to what I was doing was apparently over. "That's exactly why we decided to put it behind us," Hallie said smoothly, improvising on the spot. "Neither Gemma or I want another incident like that again."

"So embarrassing," I said with a shudder that wasn't even

entirely faked. If it hadn't been for the storm, and this sudden forced sleepover we were all having, the fact that I'd been fighting, rolling around on a boat deck getting cake shoved in my face, all the events of the day before—and the humiliation I would no doubt be feeling—would have loomed a lot larger.

"Anyway, we don't want to bother you," Hallie said as we both started to walk toward the door. "We just wanted to tell you we've taken your advice."

I gave both Karen and my dad a smile I hoped just conveyed warmth and happiness, without revealing any of the ulterior motives currently swirling around in my head.

"Girls?" Karen asked, just as we were almost to the door again. "What is this?" she was pointing at the tray on the counter.

"Oh, we just wanted to make you breakfast," Hallie said with an embarrassed shrug. "You know . . . to apologize for what we did at the party."

"It may have gotten a little damp on the walk over," I said, glancing at my dad, but then having to look away again almost immediately, sure he would be able to see through me. "But hopefully it's still edible."

"I'm sure it'll be great," Karen said, softening, as she smiled at Hallie. She believed us; I could tell. She was taking her daughter—and me—at face value. I looked quickly at my dad, who didn't look quite so accepting of this new paradigm—but he also didn't look nearly as suspicious as he had when we'd first arrived.

"Well," my dad said, crossing over to the tray and lifting the lid off it. He looked down at it, and when he looked back up at me,

I could tell he was touched—the last remaining bits of suspicion seemed to have left his face. "Gem . . . did you make us omelets?"

"Denver omelets," I said, smiling at him, all the while hoping he'd wait until we left before starting to eat. Otherwise, the plan was going to go seriously off the rails. "Your favorite."

"There's coffee there too, Mom," Hallie said, and Karen practically lunged for one of the cups on the tray. "Just—" But before she could go any further, Karen was already gulping one of the cups of coffee down. "Well, I guess you found it," Hallie said. Karen looked up from her cup, and my dad smiled down at her and wrapped his arm around her shoulders.

"Thanks so much for this, girls," he said. Though he was addressing both of us, he was looking right at me, and the trust—and happiness—in his face made my stomach clench. I looked away, not wanting to let myself see it. "Really. We appreciate the gesture."

"Won't you join us?" Karen asked, much more brightly than before, still holding on to her cup of coffee with a death grip.

"No," Hallie and I said immediately, and in unison. My dad's eyebrow's shot up, and I tried to quickly think of a plausible explanation.

"We . . . were actually in the middle of making breakfast for ourselves when we ran over here. So we have to get back to that."

"Right," Hallie said, overlapping with me as I finished. "We have, um, eggs on the stove."

"No," I said quickly, seeing both our parents' faces suddenly fill with alarm, picturing, no doubt, the fire about to break out in Bruce's professional chef's kitchen. "Not on the stove. Nothing's on the stove. Just . . . um . . ."

"I meant toast!" Hallie said quickly, with a slightly embarrassed laugh. "We have toast in the toaster."

"Well, bread in the toaster," I amended, "turning into toast. But it's probably ready by now, so we should get back to it."

Both my dad and Karen just stared at us for a moment, and I held my breath, hoping we hadn't totally revealed we were up to something. But they seemed more puzzled than anything else. "So we'll see you soon," Hallie said, giving them a big smile and reaching for the door handle.

"Bye now," I said quickly, feeling like we should make our getaway before any other questions were asked. We stepped outside, and I glanced up for just a moment at the camera perched over the guesthouse door. There was a flashing red light at the bottom of it, now that we'd activated it. But I really didn't think my dad or Karen would notice—at least, we were hoping they wouldn't.

"Okay," Hallie said when we had both made it back inside the security center, both of us wetter than before, with only one near-fall apiece. I brushed the water off my hands and took a step back from the monitors, hoping I wasn't going to drip all over the (no doubt very expensive) electronic equipment. She called up the settings on the guesthouse and then looked over at me. "Ready to do this?"

I nodded, leaning a little closer to the monitor. "Ready," I said, glancing over at her. "Heat?" I asked, and she nodded.

"It was kind of cold in there, I thought," she said. "So maybe we should start with eighty? So they can really tell the difference?"

"Do it," I said with a nod. Hallie dialed up the temperature settings to eighty and then sat back in her chair. Figuring I'd hopefully dried off enough, I sat next to her and then turned up the volume on the cameras in the guesthouse so we could hear what was happening. "How long until your mom realizes we gave her decaf?"

Hallie smiled as she leaned forward to watch the monitor. "Not long now," she said. "Caffeine headache's going to be hitting her hard, which is going to make her super-irritable."

"Good," I said. I squinted at the screen, trying to see if they'd eaten any of the breakfast. Though my dad had set out plates, it looked like they hadn't eaten anything yet. I had a feeling we would know, at least in my dad's case, when he had.

Nothing happened for a few minutes, during which Hallie and I watched the monitors like hawks. Karen drank the rest of her coffee, my dad read the paper, neither one of them speaking. I didn't want to, but I couldn't help but notice how comfortable around each other they seemed—my dad passing Karen sections of the paper without being asked, Karen taking them without looking up. I looked over at Hallie, wondering if she'd noticed this as well, only to see she was frowning at the screen, looking put out.

"What?" I asked.

"Do they just not *care* that they're letting the breakfast we made for them get cold?" she asked, staring indignantly at the screen. "Are day-old newspapers really more important than that?"

"I don't think . . ." I started, biting back a laugh, just as my dad turned to Karen and started speaking. The two of us stopped talking immediately.

"Is it warm in here?" my dad asked, turning to Karen and wiping his hand across his face.

"I don't know," Karen snapped, then a moment later, she clapped her hand over her mouth. "I'm sorry, hon," she said, shaking her head. "I just have this massive headache. Mind if I have some of your coffee?"

"Sure," my dad said, pushing his mug across the table to her. "It's too hot for coffee. You're really not noticing this?"

"I'm fine," Karen said as she picked up my dad's coffee cup and then took a long drink. "Nice of the girls to do this for us, don't you think?"

I drew in a breath as I waited for my dad's response. "Maybe," he finally said, and Hallie shot me a sharp look.

"What does maybe mean?" Hallie asked in a voice slightly above a whisper, like she was worried my dad and Karen could hear us.

"I don't know," I said back, not letting my eyes leave the screen. I also wasn't speaking at full volume. Now that we could hear my dad and Karen talking, it seemed like they could somehow also hear us, even though I knew it wasn't logical at all.

"It's just that whenever Gemma made me breakfast, she

always seemed to want something," my dad was saying to Karen. "But I can't imagine what it would be in this case."

"Maybe you could believe your daughter," Karen said, her voice still a little sharp. She frowned down at her coffee cup, like she was just now putting together that something was off about it.

"I used to," my dad said, his voice sad and quiet, and I sat back in my chair, feeling like someone had just squeezed my heart. This, I was realizing much too late, was the problem with eavesdropping—you couldn't control what you did or didn't hear. You had to be willing to hear all of it, no matter how hurtful—or honest.

"Let's just eat," Karen said, her voice still sharp.

"Good idea," my dad said with the air of someone who was happy to have a change of subject. "This looks . . . edible."

"What!" Hallie yelped from the seat next to me, apparently no longer worried about her volume at all.

"You need to stop caring so much about the breakfast part of this," I pointed out to her. "You know the objective of this was not to make them a really great meal."

"I know," Hallie said a little huffily, crossing her arms over her chest. "I just don't think he's giving us the credit we deserve, that's all."

"He's not supposed to like it," I pointed out, feeling like maybe Hallie had lost sight of why we were doing this in the first place. "Remember?" Hallie nodded grudgingly, and we both leaned forward to watch as our parents started eating. I couldn't help but wish there was a zoom function we knew how to operate.

"You're sure about this, right?" Hallie asked after a few seconds of uneventful chewing had gone on with no disastrous results, just our parents eating eggs and passing each other the salt.

"I'm sure," I said, my eyes fixed on my dad's face. "Just give it a minute." As far back as I could remember, it had been part of going out to eat with my dad—he was always checking that there was no paprika in anything being served, because he was allergic. And then, since waiters apparently sometimes didn't check, didn't care, or didn't believe him, there was the fallout that happened when he did accidentally consume some—the huge, red hives that started appearing all over his face and neck. It wasn't dangerous at all—not like some of those food allergies where you needed to carry around a special shot, or whatever—it just made him miserable and short-tempered and itchy, which was absolutely perfect for our purposes. So when we were making the omelet, I'd made sure to load it up with paprika, and then I'd doubled the amount of pepper and salt, hoping my dad wouldn't be able to taste it until he'd at least had a few bites.

"Gemma, I don't think this is working—" Hallie said just as my dad put his fork down and started scratching at his neck.

"Bingo," I said, noticing the large hives starting to appear all over my dad's face.

"Ugh," Hallie said, making a face as she leaned back from the monitors, like this might be contagious.

"Hopefully your mom will feel the same way," I said.

"Paul?" Karen asked, looking up in alarm at my dad, whose whole face was now pink and angry-looking. "Are you okay?"

My dad picked up his knife and squinted at his reflection in it, then groaned and started scratching his neck again. "It's paprika," he said. "Your daughter must have put some in the eggs. I'm allergic to it."

"*My* daughter?" Karen asked, her voice going sharp again immediately. If this morning had taught me anything so far, it was never to bother Karen before she'd had her required caffeine allotment. "How do you know this wasn't Gemma?"

"Because Gemma knows better," my dad said, his voice growing equally sharp. "She wouldn't have done this. And for the last time, in God's name, *why* is it so hot in here?"

"Just turn the temperature down if it bothers you so much," Karen snapped. "Don't just keep complaining about it."

"Oh, I'm sorry," my dad shot back, his voice dripping with sarcasm. "Is my allergic reaction *inconveniencing* you?"

"This is great," Hallie said to me, and I nodded. It was—this was what we wanted, after all. This was the means to an end. But I was still feeling the guilt twist in my stomach, especially when I remembered how peaceful and happy my dad and Karen had seemed only a few minutes earlier.

"I didn't say that," Karen snapped. "Don't put words in my mouth."

My dad was scratching at his face now, and it was like, through the monitor, I could practically see his temper rising.

My dad was usually pretty even-keeled—not so much this summer, but for most of my life, it had taken him a lot to get worked up. But once he got upset about something, it was really hard for him to get out of it. He didn't shake things off easily—it was one of the things my mother seemed to complain about the most right before they decided to separate. But I could tell when my dad was letting his temper get the better of him—I was watching it happen right this minute. "Because we all know how *precious* your words are," he said, his voice still dripping in sarcasm. "We wouldn't want to deprive the world of more vampire stories."

Next to me, Hallie drew in a sharp breath, and I felt my jaw drop. I'd really not expected *that*. I'd known my dad hadn't been crazy about Karen's erotic vampire-love bestseller, *Once Bitten*, and I knew he hadn't been thrilled when he'd gotten the job to adapt the screenplay (this was, of course, before he realized the book's pseudonymous author was actually Karen). But I never thought he would have told Karen any of that. This seemed like a really low blow, and one I knew for a fact he never would have said under normal circumstances.

"Excuse me?" Karen asked, her voice low and dangerous, and even from many feet away, watching on a TV monitor, I felt myself shiver. Karen's expression was one I would never choose to be on the receiving end of, if I could avoid it.

"Oh, come on," my dad said, rubbing his hand over his cheeks, looking miserable. "You know what I mean."

"I don't think I do," Karen said, her voice cold as she crossed her arms over her chest. "But I'm wishing we'd talked about this more before we got married. I hadn't realized you thought I was a talentless hack."

"Of course I don't," my dad said, but after the tiniest of pauses. I couldn't tell if it was because of what he was saying, or because he'd been scratching at his neck and hadn't jumped in promptly enough.

Even though I wasn't even in the same room as them, it was like I could feel the tension emanating through the screen, making me glad there was a very muddy stretch of land separating us.

"This is so good," Hallie murmured, looking from my dad to Karen. It seemed to me like you could practically *see* the two of them wondering if they'd made a mistake—which was, after all, exactly what we'd wanted. "If this just continues on for a while longer, they'll be on the road to an annulment before—"

"Hello?"

Both Hallie and I looked around, panic-stricken, before I realized the greeting was coming from the monitor.

I squinted and leaned forward, then felt my stomach plunge. Ford was walking into the guesthouse, shaking spare droplets from what looked like a gigantic golf umbrella and then leaving it by the door.

"What's Ford doing there?" Hallie asked, turning to me, like I would somehow have intel on this.

"I don't know," I said. Hallie continued to look at me, and I shook my head. "No idea," I insisted. And I really didn't know—except I had a feeling whatever he was doing there, he was going to mess up the momentum we'd just started to build.

"Morning," Ford said as he stepped into the kitchen, then stopped short when he saw my dad's face. "Uh—you okay, Paul?"

"Just allergies," my dad muttered, turning his face slightly away.

"Paprika?" Ford asked, nodding sympathetically. "Sorry to hear about that. There should be some Benadryl in the bathroom cabinet. Would that help?"

"It would," my dad said, and I could hear the relief in his voice. "Thanks." My dad headed out of the monitor frame, and I groaned. How was he supposed to have a marriage-ending fight with Karen if he was off getting allergy medicine?

"Why is it so hot in here?" Ford asked as he crossed to the thermostat, frowning. He started playing with it and then shook his head. "Were you guys really cold or something? It's set to eighty."

"No," Karen said, looking perplexed. "Paul started to complain it was too warm, but just a few minutes ago. It hasn't been like that for long."

"Huh," Ford said, and I knew him well enough that I could hear it in his voice—he was putting a puzzle together. He knew something didn't add up, and he was going to keep turning it over and over in his mind until he figured it out. "Well, it's fixed now."

"Thanks so much," Karen said.

"Anyway, I just came by to check on you guys," Ford said. "Make sure all is going okay."

"Coffee," Karen blurted out, and then I could see her face start to turn red. "I mean," she said, looking down at her mug,

"I think I need some more. With all the caffeine in it. The coffee Gemma and Hallie brought us is a little . . . weak. Do you have any at the main house?"

"Sure," Ford said, his frown deepening. "But I thought I saw . . ." I suddenly realized we'd left out the decaf we'd brewed that morning, and judging by Ford's expression, he was starting to put this together as well. "There should be some in here," he said as he crossed to one of the kitchen cabinets, opened it, and started rummaging around.

"I swear, I feel better already," my dad said as he came back into the room, looking much less irritated than he'd just been. "That stuff is a miracle." His hives still looked the same, but they must have felt better, since he was no longer itching them like crazy.

"How did you end up eating it?" Ford asked as he hauled down what looked like a Nespresso machine and a box of coffee pods. He set them on the counter, and Karen practically hugged the machine before firing it up. "You're usually so careful."

"The girls made us breakfast this morning," my dad said with a shrug, and I felt myself breathe out a tiny sigh of relief that he didn't seem suspicious about this yet, not really. "And Hallie must have put some in the eggs by accident."

"Hallie," Ford echoed, nodding, though I could tell from his voice that he wasn't entirely buying this. "Right."

"Coffee's brewing," Karen said, letting out a sigh of relief and crossing over to my dad. "How are you feeling, hon?"

"Better," my dad said as he leaned down and gave her a kiss, and Hallie and I both groaned and looked away.

"Well, that didn't work." Hallie sighed, sitting back in her chair.

"If Ford hadn't come in when he had . . ." I said, stealing a glance at the monitor again as Ford waved good-bye and headed out. "They were actually fighting. It was working."

"I know," Hallie said, and I could hear in her voice the same thing I was feeling—the terrible sense we'd gotten really close to what we needed to happen, only to have it snatched away at the last minute. "But at least they don't know it was us."

"Yeah," I said. "That's—" My words died in my throat when an image of Ford suddenly filled the camera that filmed the outside of the guesthouse. He was looking up at it, and I had a feeling he was noticing what my dad and Karen hadn't—the red blinking light that told you the camera was on. Ford looked right into the camera—and I sat back, because it was like he was looking right at me, even though I knew he couldn't see me. But it was all too clear from his expression—we were busted.

CHAPTER 11

"**D**o you think Ford's going to say anything?" Hallie half whispered to me as we crossed the foyer, walking double time, both of us trying to look natural and like we hadn't just been spying on people using security cameras. "To our parents?"

"I don't think so," I said, hoping even as I said it that it would be true. But I honestly wasn't sure. Ford had made his position on what we were doing clear, and I didn't think we'd be lucky enough to have had him suddenly change his mind in the last few hours. "But I don't think he's happy about it." Even if Ford hadn't talked to me earlier, the expression on his face when he'd looked up at the camera would have been enough to let me know just how he was feeling about it.

"Well, this isn't any of his business," Hallie said, but I could tell this was mostly bluster. This was his house, and these were his guests we were currently torturing—in that respect, it *was* his business.

"We'll just have to try something else later," I said, dropping my voice as we got closer to the living room. Hallie and I had been the only ones awake when we'd started our preparations that morning, but I could hear other voices, people moving around, and knew the time when we could talk openly about our Reverse Parent Trap plans had now come to a close. "Keep moving forward, try to capitalize on the momentum the best we can."

"My mom really freaked out when your dad talked about her books," Hallie said slowly.

I nodded. "I thought that was a pretty harsh thing for him to say," I said. "Even if he was kind of pushed to it."

"My mom's really sensitive about those books, you know," Hallie said, after glancing quickly around to make sure we wouldn't be overheard. "I mean, they make a ton of money, but everyone makes fun of the writing, and it bothers her. She knows they aren't great literature, but she gets really upset when people say things about them."

"Well . . ." I started, trying to think back to the offhand comments I'd heard my father making about *Once Bitten*, mostly before he knew who the author was, but sometimes after as well. I knew it wasn't really personal—my dad had ranted about every writer whose book he'd ever adapted. It was just part of his process. But Karen wouldn't necessarily know that. "How upset would your mom get if she heard my dad talking about her books?"

"Probably very," Hallie said. "But it's not like we can just get him to start talking. And he'd never do it if he thought she would hear—"

"Exactly," I said, realizing all at once that Gwyneth's documentary might actually turn out to be helpful for the first time all summer.

"Exactly what?" Hallie asked, sounding baffled.

I took a breath to answer her just as Reid passed us by, this time wearing a *Nightmare of the Zombuguana* promotional sweat shirt for the movie of Bruce's that had lost the most money and had nearly bankrupted the studio in the process. "Morning," Reid said cheerfully, waving at us. "Everyone sleep well?"

"Sure," I said immediately, just as Hallie said, "Fine."

"Not me," Reid said, even though he was still smiling. "I'm actually not a *huge* fan of thunder. And so every time I heard it, I was wide-awake. I'm actually pretty tired right now."

I just blinked at Reid, trying to reconcile what he was saying with the fact that he seemed blissfully happy—until Sophie descended the main staircase to join us, and his smile widened.

"Morning," she said, smiling at all of us, and at Reid a beat longer than anyone else. "I guess the house is still standing, so that's good, right? How are you guys doing?"

"Great," Reid said, taking a step closer to her, then hesitating and taking two steps back, then seeming to gather his courage and take another step forward—which basically put him exactly where he'd started. "I'm so great. How are you? Did you eat yet? Do you want some coffee?"

"Sure," Sophie said, meeting my eyes for a second and giving me a smile before turning back to Reid. "Gem? Hallie? Coffee?"

"Great," I said. Hallie nodded and, without discussing it,

I knew we were both trying to do the same thing—get Reid and Sophie out of the way so we could continue our discussion. It was only after they'd departed for the kitchen, Sophie starting to describe the dream she'd had while Reid listened, enraptured, that it hit me how well I was able to read Hallie. I wasn't sure if it was from paying crazy-close attention to what she was doing and thinking all summer—first, from when I was trying to find out if she really knew who I was when I'd been pretending to be Sophie, and then from trying to figure out what her next move might be in our revenge war. Or maybe it was just that we'd known each other for a really long time now, since we were kids. But whatever it was, it was like I was able to see what she was thinking—and I had a feeling it was going both ways.

"What were you saying?" Hallie asked, once Sophie and Reid had disappeared in the direction of the kitchen.

"I was saying . . ." I started, just as Josh emerged from the living room, yawning.

"Morning," he said, giving both of us a nod. I noticed the way his normally neat hair was sticking up in funny tufts in the back, like he'd slept on it wrong. It made him look much less intimidating and perfect than he normally did—more like the Josh I'd gotten to know in the beginning of the summer.

"Hey," I said, and Hallie just frowned at her brother.

"Josh, we're in the middle of something here," she said.

"I know," he said, folding his arms across his chest as he looked between the two of us. "That's what worries me."

"There's nothing to be worried about," Hallie said quickly, but even I could hear how false this sounded. "Fine," she relented with a sigh after a moment, when Josh was still looking at her evenly, his gaze not wavering. "Gemma and I are working together. We're trying to split up Mom and Paul."

"Hallie," Josh said, his tone big-brother disapproving. "You're doing *what*?" He looked at me, and I felt my cheeks get hot.

"Oh, come on," Hallie said, then glanced around quickly and lowered her voice. "You're telling me you want this? You're telling me you think it's a good idea for all of us to be stuck together forever?"

Josh glanced at me for a moment before he looked down at the ground and shook his head. "No," he said. "But I still think this is Mom's choice to make. Not yours."

"All we're doing is attempting to show them that they might run into problems down the road," I said, aware even as I said it that this was stretching the truth, at best. Josh raised an eyebrow at me, and I made myself look away, sure that if he kept on looking at me like that, I would admit everything we were up to.

"Don't tell Mom," Hallie said, narrowing her eyes at her brother. "Josh? Promise?"

Josh looked between us for a moment and then shook his head. "I want to stay as far away from all this as possible," he said. "I don't think anything good can come from the two of you teaming up."

Even though I knew why he was saying this, hearing it was hard—like someone had just pressed on a bruise. "Well . . ." I started, glancing over at Hallie. She was looking down at the ground, biting her lip, and maybe feeling the same thing I was.

"Really," Josh said, shaking his head. "I'm done with this. Just going to get some breakfast. Leave me out of whatever schemes you guys are cooking up, okay?" He turned and walked toward the kitchen, and for just a moment I watched him go.

I had a hollow feeling in my stomach, and all I wanted was to be able to somehow fast-forward a few months into the future, when my dad and Karen had gotten their quickie marriage annulled, Hallie and I were out of each other's lives, and everyone was that much happier. Then Josh—and Ford and Sophie—would see we'd done this for the right reasons.

"Anyway," Hallie said, turning back to me with the air of someone who wanted to ignore what had just happened. She leaned closer, and I could see she didn't want to discuss what Josh had said, or question if we were doing the right thing. I realized in that moment excatly how Hallie had been able to pull off what she had—the five-year revenge plan against me she'd executed to perfection. When there was something she wanted, she didn't let anything shake her from her path. "You were saying?"

"Right," I said, trying to gather up my thoughts. "Yes. So. I think we need to make sure your mom sees just what my dad really thinks about her books—needs to hear him saying the words."

"I understood that part," Hallie said, frowning at me. "I just didn't understand how you thought we were going to be able to pull it off."

"Gwyneth's documentary," I said more quietly than ever, even though we were alone in the foyer (well, except for the polar bear, but I wasn't sure he counted). "She had all of us wearing cameras."

"Including your dad?" Hallie asked, and I could see she was starting to understand what I was getting at.

"*Especially* my dad," I said. "This started out as a documentary about Bruce, after all."

Hallie looked at me, a small smile starting to take over her face. "That could really work," she said slowly.

"We're just going to have to go through a lot of footage," I said, wincing. Even a few days ago, I would have felt bad about going through Gwyneth's footage, possibly messing with her documentary. But that moment had long since passed.

"That's okay," Hallie said, and I could see she was really warming to this idea. "There's probably great stuff in there. And then it won't even be anything we're doing—we'll just be holding a mirror up to the problems that are already there."

I nodded. I knew this wasn't exactly the truth, but it was close enough, and besides, it really did seem like our best bet if we wanted to break our parents up before we lost this close-quarters opportunity. "All the footage is in the editing suite upstairs," I said. "Gwyneth converted one of the closets." I hadn't ever thought I'd be grateful Gwyneth skipped town, leaving the rest of us to deal with the fallout, but now I couldn't be happier about it. I knew if she were here, she never would have let any of us near her precious equipment or the footage she'd been assembling over the last month.

"Okay," Hallie said, nodding. "So let's—"

"Gem?" I turned around to see Ford standing across the

foyer, in the doorway of the kitchen, not looking too happy. "Can I talk to you a second?"

I glanced back at Hallie, who clearly wanted to get started on this right away. I did too, but felt like I owed Ford an explanation—even though I had a feeling he'd already figured out our part in things. "Top of the stairs," I said to her under my breath. "Fourth door on the right. It should be open, and I'm pretty sure all the files are labeled."

"Got it," Hallie said just as quietly back to me as she turned and headed for the staircase.

I turned back to Ford and started to walk toward him, not liking at all how guilty I was feeling as I looked at him. Somehow he didn't even have to say anything—the look in his eyes was enough. "Hey," I said as Ford walked a few more steps into the kitchen, and I followed. "Look, about this morning—" I stopped short when I realized the kitchen was otherwise occupied—Josh was rummaging around in the cabinets, and Reid and Sophie were sitting at the kitchen counter, Sophie eating what was her favorite breakfast: cold pizza. (We'd had numerous arguments about this, since I was convinced cold pizza was an abomination, not to mention a slap in the face of the inventor of the microwave.) As I looked around at everyone, I couldn't help but think there were just a few too many people in the house, and they were all really getting in the way of the secret conversations I kept trying to have.

"Do you guys have any cereal?" Josh asked, glancing over at us as he shut one of the cabinet doors.

"Sure," Ford said immediately. "Upper left."

Josh shook his head. "Tried that," he said. "Nada."

I felt myself frown. I'd helped myself to some of that cereal only a few hours before, when Hallie and I were on omelet attempt number two, and all the cooking was starting to make me hungry. "It should be there." I'd had a bowl, but Hallie hadn't wanted any, so it wasn't like we'd polished off the box or anything.

"Yeah," Ford said. "I just had some earlier. It's up there." Josh pulled open the cabinet again, and I looked too, but it was a cereal-free zone. "Huh," Ford said after a moment. "Well, maybe someone else finished the box." I could hear the doubt in his voice as he spoke, though, and I was feeling it too. Hallie hadn't had any, Ford had put the box back after he'd finished, and Reid or Sophie would have spoken up if they'd taken it, right?

I did a quick head count and realized the only person who really wasn't accounted for was Teddy. That was probably it—he'd come by the kitchen and had just taken the box with him, for some reason, probably back to his meditation room. Maybe it was just habit, collecting food in bulk and taking it with him, after all that time being chained to the bulldozer.

"No worries," Josh said with a shrug. "I'll heat up some pizza."

"Thank you," I said immediately, and Sophie looked across the kitchen and shook her head at me.

"You and your anti–cold pizza stance," Ford said, giving me a smile. I smiled back at him, but a moment later it was like he remembered he was unhappy with me, and his smile faded. He tipped his head toward the living room, and I nodded, and we walked there together in silence. It really seemed like, in a house as big as this one was, it should have been easier to find places to talk in private, but that was really proving not to be the case.

Thankfully, the living room was empty, and Ford turned on the light switch, the lights coming on but flickering every few seconds. "Listen," I said quickly, trying to get in front of this.

"Paprika?" Ford asked skeptically, raising an eyebrow at me. "Decaf coffee? Turning up the heat?"

I felt my cheeks get hot. I knew Ford had seen through what we were trying to do, but that didn't necessarily mean I wanted it thrown back in my face. "Here's the thing," I said, "we were just trying to—"

"Oh, I know what you were trying to do," Ford said as he crossed his arms over his chest. "I'm just disappointed, that's all. I thought we talked about it."

"We did," I said, trying not to let Ford see just how deeply the word *disappointed* had hurt me. "But Hallie and I are just trying to prevent them from getting hurt in the future. That's all."

"Really," Ford said, his dark eyes not leaving mine. This was one of the best things about Ford, but also one I didn't love being on the other end of—he would call you on it when you made mistakes, and not pull any punches when he told you so. "So this—this thing you and Hallie are doing—it's just for your parents' benefit. Nothing else."

With almost anyone else, I would have been able to give some half-truth, talk my way out of this. But I couldn't do that with

Ford. Not only would he be able to see through this immediately, but I didn't want to lie to him. He was the one person who had known all my secrets and kept on standing by me. I knew that was not a person I should start lying to. "No," I finally admitted, the truth at the bottom of everything Hallie and I were doing, even as we might pretend we were doing it selflessly. We were doing this because *we* didn't want to be unhappy, not because we were worried about our parents' future unhappiness. That was part of it, I knew, but it wasn't the primary reason. I looked up at Ford, and saw he wasn't jumping in with a speech of his own, wasn't about to tell me *I told you so* or give me a lecture. He was just there, waiting, listening, ready to hear me when I figured out what I wanted to say. "I guess . . ." I started haltingly, just as my phone rang in my pocket.

Figuring it was just Hallie, lost on her way to the editing suite, and planning to ignore it if it was, I pulled the phone out of my pocket—only to see Rosie's contact picture flashing back at me. "It's Rosie," I said to Ford, and he nodded.

"We'll talk later," he said, giving me that half-smile and touching my arm for the briefest of moments before he headed out of the living room again.

"Rosie?" I asked as I answered the phone, even though my thoughts were focused on the moment of Ford's fingertips grazing my arm, trying to figure out what, if anything, it meant. It was probably just a friendly gesture, right? But in the past, Ford's friendly gestures had been limited to things like bear hugs. Nothing so small—and somehow more intimate—as an arm brush.

"Gem," Rosie said. At least I was pretty sure that was what she said. There was so much static on the line, it was sounding like she was calling me from the bottom of a well. "Just . . . wanted to check . . ."

"What?" I asked, pressing the phone to my ear harder. "I lost you there for a second."

"The *generator*," Rosie said, and with that one word, I remembered, all at once. *That* was the thing I'd forgotten to do, the thing that had been dancing on the edge of my memory last night. "Did you do it?"

"Right," I said immediately, feeling my heart start to pound. I thought back to the very detailed list of instructions for what I had to do, folded up in my hoodie pocket. I turned to run for my room, taking the steps two at a time. "I'm on it."

"But have you done it?" Rosie asked, our connection now crystal clear for some reason, so I could hear the worry in her voice.

"Just going to double-check it against your instructions," I said, which, I reasoned as I hurried down the hall to my room, wasn't *entirely* a lie. "Gotta go, Rosie. I'll call you back soon." I hung up then, turned the ringer to silent, and put my phone in the back pocket of my jeans. I grabbed the list out of my hoodie— and then also grabbed my hoodie for good measure, since it was really getting chilly—and headed down the stairs as fast as I'd come up them. Because even though I'd just glanced at the note again, one glance had been enough to remind me of the scariest part of Rosie's instructions—if the generator lost power, there would be no way to restore it again until the regular power got turned back on. Basically, if I let the generator run out of fuel, we would be stuck in the dark until all the Hamptons got its power back. And that was something I didn't want to have to depend on.

When I made it to the bottom of the stairs, I pulled out the list again when I realized I wasn't entirely sure where I needed to go. There it was, right at the top—*propane tanks for generator are located in the garage.* I folded up the list again and took off at a run.

CHAPTER 12

I flipped the switch to turn on the light in the garage, praying as I did so that this had been hooked up to the generator as well. It took a second, but then the lights flickered on—not all of them, but most—and I let myself breathe a sigh of relief as I squinted at the paper again and glanced around the garage, wishing I knew exactly what a propane tank looked like or that we had access to the Internet so I could find out information like this.

I shivered as I looked around the dimly lit garage. The equipment looked pretty ominous in the flickering overhead light—these huge pieces of machinery, taking up the whole space, stretching as tall as the ceiling. There was what looked like a small crane, a steamroller, a truck, a backhoe, my ex-boyfriend . . .

I jumped when I realized I had just seen a person sitting on the backhoe. A person I recognized. "Teddy?" I asked, baffled, as I took a step closer to him.

"Oh, hi, Gemma," he said, from where he was sitting in the driver's seat, like this was just a totally normal place for me to find him hanging out. "How are you doing?"

For just a second I thought about telling him the truth—that I had teamed up with my former archnemesis and we were plotting to destroy our parents' new marriage, even though there was a piece of me that wasn't sure this was the best idea—but only for a second, before I dismissed it. I had to find some propane tanks and make sure the generator was filled, and not explain my current mental state to Teddy. "I'm okay," I finally said. "What are you doing here?"

Teddy let out a long sigh and gave the side of the backhoe a fond pat. "I needed to reconnect with my recent past," he said. "As part of my meditative journey. And I spent a lot of time with this fella. It seemed the right place to go."

"Right," I said, realizing after a moment that this was the backhoe Teddy had chained himself to. "So, where's the cereal?"

"What?" Teddy asked. "I don't know what you're talking about."

"Sure," I said. If he'd stolen the cereal—and there was dairy or preservatives in it—I knew he'd never admit it. I looked closer at Teddy in the flickering light and saw there were dark circles under his eyes, and he looked tired and pale. Maybe it was his walkabout taking it out of him. But I knew all too well what it looked like when you were struggling to accept a breakup. And Teddy, right now, bore a very close resemblance to what I'd looked like in the beginning of the summer, right after he'd broken my heart. "Um," I said. Teddy looked down at me, and I had to glance away, not sure I was going to be able to have this conversation if I had to look at him.

"What?" he asked. After a second he clambered down from the backhoe and stood on the garage floor next to me.

"I . . ." I said, still not quite able to believe I was really going to say this. Of all the twists this summer had taken, this development might have been the most surprising. "How are you feeling about the breakup? Is your vision quest bringing you clarity?"

Teddy let out a sigh. "Not as yet," he said. "But . . . you know, I'm just beginning. I should really be fasting for this to work."

"Please don't," I said immediately. The last thing we needed in the midst of all this was for Teddy to pass out from hunger while it was impossible for ambulances to get through.

"Hallie . . ." Teddy said, like he was turning her name over in his head. "It is what it is," he said, and I could tell he was trying to sound like he was blasé and over it, but it was a very bad acting job, and one that made me glad he'd never tried out for any of the school plays, especially since Teddy wasn't the greatest at handling rejection. For just a moment I wondered if I'd been this transparent when I'd been crushed by our breakup but was pretending not to be, but then I realized a moment later I probably had. "But," he said, taking a step closer to me, "I mean, have you thought about what we talked about yesterday? You know . . . maybe getting back together?"

I took a step away, in the guise of pretending to look for the propane tank—even though I still wasn't sure what exactly I was supposed to be looking for. Was it like a military tank? That didn't make any sense, did it? But really, I was stalling, as I needed to organize my thoughts. I never would have thought the ending of my story with Teddy would happen like this—the two of us talking in a garage while a storm raged outside. But I also knew I needed to put an end to us once and for all. "Teddy," I said, making my voice gentle but firm, "we're not getting back together."

Teddy blinked at me. "Oh," he said. He tilted his head to the side. "Is this because you don't want to be, like, the rebound?" he asked. "You wouldn't be, I promise!"

"No," I said, trying not to let myself sound exasperated. "It has nothing to do with that."

"But you wanted to get back together," he pointed out, in his reasonable voice, like maybe the reason I wasn't jumping at this chance was just that I'd forgotten about this. "Remember? Outside the pizza parlor?"

"I remember," I said. "But that was a really long time ago."

"It was the beginning of the summer," Teddy shot back, and I blinked at him, realizing he was right. But it felt like longer than that. It felt like an entire lifetime ago. Before I could try to explain, Teddy crossed his arms over his chest. "Is this about Ford?"

"No," I said immediately, then felt my face get hot. "What do you mean?"

"I'm not blind, you know," he said with a shrug. "I can see there's something going on with you two."

"There's actually not," I said, realizing as I said it that it was the truth. The truth of it was, Ford and I were friends, and nothing concrete had ever really happened with us, other than a kiss that was now almost four years old. I had all these confusing feelings for him, but despite the algorithm, I had no proof he felt the same way about me.

"But you always liked him," Teddy said, now sounding more than a little irritated. "Even when we were together. I could tell by the way you talked about him."

"Listen," I said, feeling very acutely that the last thing I wanted to do was to debate my feelings about Ford with Teddy. "Let's leave Ford out of this for the moment. Us not being together has nothing do with that."

"Then what is it?" Teddy asked, sounding genuinely confused as he stuck his hands in his pockets. "You wanted to get back together, and now I'm single again so we *can* get back together—I don't understand what the problem is."

"Because everything's different now," I said, hearing my voice rise, echoing off the metal of the machinery that surrounded us. "I mean, yes, it's only been two months. But so much has changed, Teddy. People's feelings don't just stay the same."

"Mine did," he said, but even as he was speaking, I was shaking my head.

"No, they didn't," I said. Teddy looked at me incredulously, and I wasn't sure if this was because I was questioning what he was saying or that I was questioning him at all—when we'd been together, I'd been happy to follow along with him. I almost never disagreed with him this much or questioned his judgment—which was one of the many reasons I knew we shouldn't get back together. "I'm just familiar," I said with a shrug, remembering what Teddy had told me on the boat at Hallie's party. "And like you said, you miss who you were when we were together. But you don't really miss *me*."

"Yes, I do," Teddy insisted, and I could see the familiar stubbornness in his face, the one that showed up when he was sure a restaurant was serving him gluten when he'd specifically requested otherwise, or he was sure he could get someone to sign his latest petition if only he talked to them a little bit longer.

"You don't," I said. "Because I don't think you really even know me." As I said it, I felt just how true it was. I had been so dazzled by Teddy, I had put my real self aside to fit into his world, molding myself into Teddy Callaway's perfect girlfriend, putting my own likes and dislikes in a drawer for the two years we were a couple. Even though it hadn't really been that long since we'd been together, there was a piece of me that still couldn't believe I'd done this. It was a me I wasn't exactly proud of, and one I really didn't want to go back to.

"Gemma, that's crazy," Teddy said, staring at me. I could tell he believed this—but he was wrong. Mostly because I'd never made him see otherwise. "Of course I know you. Don't be silly."

"I'm not," I insisted, hearing my voice rise again, and I knew, somehow, that even though this wasn't how or where I would have chosen to do this, Teddy and I needed to have this out. That we'd needed to say these things to each other for a while now. "And it's partially my own fault, because I just went along with you. But I actually don't like vegan food. I hate documentaries on the plight of the worker. And about the marsh warbler—"

"What about it?" Teddy said, looking like he was afraid of the answer.

"I walked into that meeting by accident," I said, thinking back to the first time we'd met, Teddy in an empty classroom, organizing a club for the protection of the (actually fairly ugly) bird. I'd been lost, just looking for a quiet place to call Sophie to see if she could find me. But there had been Teddy, and I'd gotten an immediate crush on him. And so I'd pretended I cared about what he cared about, just to keep staying in his presence. Well, those days were over. "I actually don't care about the warbler like you do."

Teddy just looked at me for a long moment and then took a seat on a nearby workbench, like he needed to be sitting while he processed all this. "Oh," he finally said.

"Sorry to tell you like this," I said after the silence between us threatened to move into awkward territory. "I . . . just thought you should know."

"No, it's good," he said, his voice hollow, which seemed to contradict what he was saying. "I'm just learning that all my relationships have been total shams, so that's good to know."

"Come on," I said, shaking my head, but Teddy was talking over me.

"No, it's true," he said. "First I learn Hallie was just using me to get back at you, and then you tell me you were just pretending to care about the things I cared about."

"Your relationship with Hallie wasn't a sham," I said, going over to sit next to him on the end of the workbench. I couldn't quite believe I was doing this—if you'd told me at the beginning of the summer I'd be trying to talk Teddy into getting back with the girl who'd stolen him from me, I wouldn't have believed it for anything. But the facts were undeniable—I thought about how terrified Hallie had been that I'd tell Teddy how they really got together, and her blotchy face last night . . . She'd been crying, even if she didn't want to admit it. As much as I might have wanted it to be otherwise, Hallie and Teddy had had something real between them. "She really cares about you. I think she's taking the breakup hard."

Teddy shrugged, but I could see on his face that this was affecting him. And I suddenly realized that was probably one of the reasons he was trying to get back together with me—rather than actually feeling the hurt of his breakup, he was just trying to push past it and move on. "I . . . Are you sure there's no chance you guys could get back together?"

Teddy let out a short laugh as he looked over at me. "You're trying to get us back together?" he asked, eyebrows raised. "Really?"

"I know," I said with a small laugh of my own. "It's weird."

"Of course we can't get back together," he said after a moment. "She *lied* to me."

"Well, you lied to me," I shot back at him, not even realizing I was still holding on to this anger until it was spilling out of me. Teddy looked over at me, his expression confused, and I went on, "When you were *cheating* on me with Hallie? Remember that?"

"Oh," Teddy said, a blush coloring his cheeks. "Right. I'm really sorry about that, Gemma."

"Thank you," I said. I hadn't realized how much I'd needed to hear that until he was saying it. I took a breath and let it out, trying to see what I was feeling. And I realized . . . I was over it. It had taken the better part of the summer, but I wasn't upset about it any longer. "Look, I'm willing to forgive you for what you did," I said, and Teddy looked over at me, surprised. "And I think that means you should think about forgiving Hallie."

Teddy shook his head. "I don't think I can do that."

I just wanted to say this, and then I would leave Teddy and Hallie to their own devices. "Think about it," I said. "I actually think you two are a good match for each other. Better than you and I ever were." Teddy looked up at me sharply, and I gave him a small sad shrug. "Why not give it another shot? You two can start fresh, being honest with each other this time." Teddy just looked at me, and it was like I could see him considering this. The sureness that had been in his eyes before seemed to be wavering. "Just think about it," I added, and after a long moment, "you know, on your walkabout."

Teddy gave me a small nod. "Okay," he said, and I gave him a half-smile. "What do you think?" he asked, suddenly sounding nervous. "You and I—can we be friends?"

I thought about it. Teddy and I had never been friends—we'd met, I'd developed a massive crush, we'd started dating, and I'd spent two years pretending to love tempeh. But why not? We were here together, having this conversation, so maybe anything was possible. "We can try," I said, and Teddy smiled at me.

"That's great," he said. "Because—"

Before he could continue, my phone beeped with a text. I pulled it out of my pocket and looked down at the screen, feeling my eyes widen as I read it.

Hallie Bridges

Hey. Think I found something. Meet me in video room ASAP.

CHAPTER 13

"**O**kay," Hallie said as she leaned forward, squinting at the screen. "I think it was . . . Wait, hold on a sec. I just had it." I looked over at her, wondering why I'd full-out run from the garage for this. Though, honestly, I had been happy to have an excuse to leave Teddy. We'd both said what we needed to say, and now it was up to him to decide what he wanted to do. But I did find I felt a bit lighter now than I had before—like we'd both cleared the air and now might actually be able, against all odds, to be something resembling friends.

I watched the monitor as Hallie fast-forwarded through what looked like an endless clip of the pool, going around in circles—I had a feeling we were in Bruce's POV cam, as pacing around the pool while screaming at his interns was pretty much Bruce's MO. "Can you even go through these without being online?" I asked.

"Yeah," Hallie said as she clicked a button, and I was looking at Rosie shaking her head and laughing as she typed on her

BlackBerry. "All her files were stored on this computer. It looks like only about half of them were organized by whose camera it was, though. So we might have to sift through a lot of footage to find stuff that hasn't been labeled. And I was going through your dad's when I found something—but now it's gone again. Just hold on."

"Holding," I said, having to look away from the screen because all the fast-forwarding was starting to make me dizzy. I honestly had no idea how Gwyneth had looked at this stuff for hours and hours every day. I glanced at Hallie for a second, wondering if I should tell her about the conversation I'd just had with Teddy. After a moment, though, I decided against it. After all, maybe nothing would come of it on Teddy's end, and then I would have gotten her hopes up for nothing. I leaned back in my chair, looking around at the editing suite.

It had been a room none of us had been allowed to spend much time in when Gwyneth was working here, as she'd pretty much taken it over and claimed it as her domain. There was a large computer monitor, as well as state-of-the-art editing and sound-mixing equipment, since when Bruce found out his daughter had an interest in following him into the family business, he had spared no expense in getting her set up professionally. Whenever I'd been in here and Gwyneth was working, she'd always encouraged us not to touch anything and to leave her alone to work as much as possible. Which had been pretty annoying when I'd thought she was just making a documentary about Bruce. But it made sense now that I knew she'd switched her focus so the documentary was about me and

Hallie. She probably hadn't wanted anyone—especially me—to pick up on the fact that she'd changed the subject matter.

My phone beeped with a text, and I pulled it out, surprised to see it was from, of all people, Gwyneth.

Gwyneth Davidson
Hey! How's it going?

I started to write back, but I saw the three little dots in Gwyneth's text bubble flashing, meaning she was already writing again, and asking me how I was had just been a rhetorical question, not something she actually expected an answer to.

Gwyneth Davidson
How's the storm? Looks crazy on TV! Hope everyone's okay!

Gwyneth Davidson
I just wanted to make sure that while I'm gone, nobody messes with my equipment or footage. If you wouldn't mind keeping an eye out, and staying away from it, I'd appreciate it! Would hate for anything to get damaged or compromised! Xoxoxo

"What?" Hallie asked, glancing over at me and seeing me looking down at my phone.

"Text from Gwyneth," I said, holding out the screen so she could read it. "Weird, right?"

Hallie shrugged. "I'm sure it's just a coincidence," she said. She shook her head. "I really can't believe the nerve of her, though—she runs away but then wants to make sure you're not going to touch her stuff while she's gone."

"Yeah," I agreed, shaking my head as well. Not that I wanted to damage Gwyneth's very expensive equipment—but I felt pretty strongly that she'd given up her right to ask us for favors the moment she'd hopped on a plane to Los Angeles.

"Oh wait, I found it," Hallie said, stopping scrolling. "I think it was on Bruce's assistant's camera—her name's Rosie, right?"

"Right," I said, leaning forward to look at the screen, then leaning back again immediately when my face filled the monitor. "Oh dear," I said, realizing I must have gotten in Rosie's camera range when I'd leaned past her to grab something. It also must have been early in the morning, as my eyes looked bleary, my hair was sticking up funny, and I was yawning every few seconds. It was not the best look on me. For just a moment I looked at Hallie sharply. Was this the old Hallie, the one who had spent the whole summer trying to hurt me, back again? Was she trying to show me the most unflattering footage of myself, just for fun?

"Yeah, sorry about that," Hallie said, shooting me a sympathetic look. "I can't believe all of you had to be filmed at all hours like that."

"You forget the cameras are there after a while," I admitted. When I'd heard reality stars say the same thing, when they tried to explain why they let their bad behavior be filmed, I'd never believed it. But I got it now—you really did forget that everyone was wearing cameras and they were capturing stuff like just how messy your hair looked first thing in the morning.

"Okay, here it is," Hallie said, turning up the volume. I leaned forward again, bracing myself this time just in case my giant unkempt head suddenly appeared in frame again.

"What's with the face, Paul?" I heard Rosie's voice ask as she crossed behind the kitchen cabinet to face my dad. He looked much more pulled together than I was, but he didn't look happy by any stretch of the imagination.

"This book," he said with a sigh, and he tossed aside what I could see now was a copy of *Once Bitten*—I recognized the familiar black-and-red cover. "I swear, most of it isn't even English. Whoever published this and had the temerity to call it a 'book' committed a crime against literature. And Bruce expects me to turn this into something people won't walk out of the theaters from en masse. I know he always expects miracles, but that might be asking for a little too much in this case."

Hallie paused the feed and looked over at me, a smile on her face. "Right?" she said.

"Wow," I said, letting out a low whistle. I hadn't remembered this specific conversation—but I'd known it was how my dad felt about the book, particularly when he'd just started working on it. But there was something so different about actually seeing and hearing someone say these things. It made it *so* much worse. If anything was going to split them up, it was stuff like this. "That's good."

"Thanks," Hallie said, and I could tell she was pleased with herself. "I think we should start pulling as much as we can of this kind of stuff together."

"Sounds good," I said, nodding, knowing this was our best option, even as the thought of going through weeks of our camera files wasn't exactly the most appealing way to spend an afternoon. I looked up at the screen for just a moment. The feed was frozen on my dad's face, his expression irritated and dismissive. I knew he'd thought he was having a private conversation—despite the waivers we'd all signed and the cameras he was aware we were all wearing. But he'd never intended for Karen to hear him saying these things. We weren't manipulating anything—he had said it—but for just a second I felt myself waver. Ford's words especially were reverberating in my mind.

"Gemma?" Hallie was looking at me, her brow furrowed. "You okay?"

I looked back at Hallie, and it was all the confirmation I needed. This was fine now, the two of us doing this. We were united in a common goal, after all. But the second this was over, I wasn't sure I would trust her as far as I could throw her. There was still all our history together, to say nothing of my history with Josh. The fact was, Hallie and I couldn't be sisters. It just wasn't possible. And so nipping this in the bud would just be the best thing for everyone involved, including our parents. "I'm good," I said, and I could hear the clarity and determination in my voice as I said it. I leaned forward and nodded at the monitor. "Let's do this."

our hours later, my eyes were burning, my back was aching, and I was no longer harboring any delusions (if I'd had any left) that it was fun to work in the movie business. I'd also realized I needed to brush my hair more often; most of the time when I was on people's cameras, I seemed to have just gotten out of bed or just come in from the pool or the beach. In contrast, Sophie's hair always somehow looked perfect, and I made a mental note to ask her if she was secretly combing it during her spare time, or what her trick was, because I refused to believe it was just a coincidence.

Hallie and I were surrounded by empty plates and snack wrappers—we'd been making occasional forays down to the fridge, trying to keep up the energy needed to go through massive amounts of (mostly boring) camera footage. According to the meteorologists in their foul-weather gear, the storm was holding steady—not getting massively worse, but certainly not getting better anytime soon. Everyone who wasn't currently hiding in a video suite or in a meditation room (that was, everyone but us and Teddy) had spent the afternoon stacking sandbags on the beach, coming in wet and cold and irritated. But I couldn't help but be relieved that maybe we'd kept the ocean at bay for just a little longer. And after all, the storm had to die down at some point . . . right? It couldn't go on like this forever. Maybe people had just become resigned to the inevitable, but nobody in the house seemed quite as desperate to leave as they had the day before. After the sandbagging, everyone had retreated to their separate corners—Ford was in the pool house, working on his algorithm; my dad and Karen were in the guesthouse, both trying to write; Teddy had come back from the garage and was reading in Bruce's brag room; and Josh, Sophie, and Reid were watching movies together in the living room. They were stuck with actual DVDs, though, since they didn't have access to Bruce's massive streaming library, something that seemed to annoy everyone, since most of the movies Bruce had physical copies of were either the ones he'd produced, or awards-contender screeners from a few years back. But presumably it was better than nothing, since every time I passed by the living room on a food or beverage run, they were watching something.

Hallie and I had put together a pretty devastating compilation for Karen to see. It was painful for *me* to watch, and I wasn't even directly involved. It had taken hours of sifting through footage, but we'd narrowed it down. Well, Hallie had, really. It seemed to help that she had a little bit of objectivity and hadn't been living in the house while this was going on, as I didn't have that at all. I tended to get too caught up in trying to remember on what day something had happened, or complaining about my hair, or noting the rest of the backstory on what was going on in the house that day, despite Hallie telling me over and over it didn't really matter—and then, more directly, that she didn't really care.

Since we didn't have the ability to upload anything, Hallie was going the old-fashioned route and burning a DVD of the footage. While we waited for it to finish, I stretched out my back and rubbed my eyes, and Hallie continued to scroll through footage for some reason. I for one never wanted to see myself on camera ever again, or at least not in the near future.

"Gemma!" Hallie said, snapping her fingers in front of my face, and I moved my hands away from my eyes.

"What?" I asked, squinting at the monitor. "Is it done?"

"Not quite yet," she said. "I just wanted to show you something."

"Please not Bruce walking again," I groaned as Hallie laughed. The Bruce-pool-pacing footage had the ability to make me incredibly nauseous, and Hallie had gotten a kick out of telling me she had really great footage to show me, before cueing up a sped-up section of Bruce footage.

"No," she said, shaking her head as she seemed to scroll through about six different camera feeds at once, trying to find what she was looking for. It really seemed like, after this, Hallie might have a real future as an editor. She just wouldn't be able to reveal to anyone where she'd gotten the experience. "This."

The scene we'd switched to was bright, and I realized we were in Hallie's sun-drenched kitchen. Karen was smiling at someone—presumably my dad—as she leaned across the kitchen table toward him. "Have you ever been to Pearson's Bluff?" she was asking.

"No," I heard my dad say. "But I'll go immediately. Where is it?" Even though I couldn't see him, it was like I could hear the happiness suffusing my dad's voice—it perfectly matched Karen's expression, and I bit my lip as I looked at it. Why was Hallie showing me this?

"It's at the border of Quonset and Bridgehampton," Karen said, her voice going dreamy and far away. "And it's my favorite spot in the Hamptons. Maybe even in the whole world. The most romantic spot there is—"

"Sorry," Hallie said as Karen's image froze and then disappeared. "Must have saved the wrong one. That's not what I wanted to show you."

"Oh okay," I said, nodding a few too many times, wishing I could unsee the footage she'd just shown me. I didn't want to see proof of our parents being really happy and in love, didn't want to hear about Karen's favorite spots. It would make what we were trying to do that much harder.

"Here we go," Hallie said, typing rapidly, then gesturing to the monitor.

I squinted at the screen—it took me a moment to understand what I was looking at, before I realized it was the same footage from two cameras—mine and Ford's. So on one feed, you could see me, looking at him, and on the other, you could see him, looking at me. At first it was slightly bizarre to see both videos happening at the same time, but I noticed after a second or two my eyes seemed to adjust and I got used to it.

It was night, and Ford and I were sitting next to each other out by the pool, the outdoor and pool lights providing the camera's only lighting—as a result, when either one of us moved, we were cast into shadow, until we shifted again and moved back into the light. The result was weirdly romantic, like the whole thing had been lit with mood lighting, even though it was just the result of circumstance.

Ford had his laptop out, and he was saying something that made me smile. I felt myself smiling now, just looking at him, even though the sound was off, and I had no idea what he was saying. "What did you want to show me?" I asked, trying, but failing, to take my eyes away from Ford. There was just something about him—the way his features were lit up by the soft glow from his laptop screen, the way his smiles were small and measured, the result, I knew, of a childhood spent in heavy-duty orthodontia. There was the way we seemed so comfortable with each other, the easiness between us . . .

"This," Hallie said, shaking me out of this reverie. "Watch that camera," she said, pointing to the one that Ford was on—meaning the one I'd been wearing.

"Okay," I said, leaning forward even more, wondering what I was looking for, feeling weirdly like an archaeologist in my own life.

Ford must have said something, because on his camera, I nodded and then looked out toward the water. He looked away too, but a moment later he looked back at me. He must have forgotten he was being filmed, or he didn't care, because he was looking at me, his eyes traveling over the planes of my face as I stared down at the water, totally unaware. I could feel my heart racing. Was this what I was looking for? My heart was hammering against my rib cage, and this only increased as I saw Ford draw in a breath and then reach out for me, like he was going to smooth back my hair, at the very moment I turned to face him. He brought his arm back, running his hand through his own hair, and judging from my expression, I hadn't known anything had happened—or almost happened. I didn't know the truth of it until right now.

Hallie hit pause, and I felt myself slump back against my chair. This was it. This was the proof I'd said I wanted. But . . . now what was I supposed to do about it? "Oh," I said quietly, and Hallie nodded. Suddenly I snapped out of these thoughts and back to reality. "Why would you show me that?" I asked, folding my arms, willing my mind to go to places Hallie's would. Was it for blackmail? Something to use against me later on?

"I just think you're being an idiot," she said coolly, "and much as I usually enjoy seeing that"—I rolled my eyes at her, fighting a smile—"I thought maybe you could use some definitive proof about how he feels."

"Oh," I said slowly, looking at her closely. It seemed like she was telling the truth. And try as I might, I honestly couldn't think of what her ulterior motive was here. "What were we even talking about?" I asked, nodding at the screen as I looked at the two frozen images of me and Ford, both of us looking at the other.

"Why?" Hallie asked as she scrolled back a few seconds, and Ford's hand extended and then retreated again. "Going to try to re-create the conversation?" She laughed and then turned the volume back on.

"Said Hallie was taking the SATs," Ford was saying. "But she wasn't." I drew in a sharp breath as I remembered, all at once, what this conversation was about. This had only been a few nights ago—though the thought that we were once able to sit outside, by the pool in the moonlight, and not be either soaking wet or in danger of being hit by wind-carried debris seemed impossible now. Ford's algorithm had finally come through as he'd been looking through Hallie's metadata for anything we could use to take her down. And he'd found a big one. The day Hallie had met Teddy—by accident, he thought—had been a day she knew I wouldn't be with him, since I'd posted online I was going to be taking the SATs. But Ford had shown that Hallie had claimed to take the test that day too—despite the fact that she'd spent the afternoon in Putnam, pretending to be meeting Teddy by accident.

It had been a *big* find, and I knew Ford had been happy the algorithm had dug it up—but when I said I didn't want to do anything with it, I could tell he was relieved. But we hadn't done anything with it—hadn't told anyone but each other, hadn't included it in the video we'd originally planned to show. It felt like it was crossing a line, somehow. That was the kind of stuff that got you expelled from schools and blacklisted from colleges, and I hadn't even wanted to go near something that had those kinds of serious, life-ruining consequences.

Ford was going on, explaining just how he'd discovered this, and I reached across Hallie and paused the feed, figuring she didn't need to hear this. She'd gone white as a ghost, her eyes huge as she stared at the monitor. "Look . . ." I started after a moment of Hallie still staring at the frozen image in silence. "I—"

"Were you just waiting for the right time?" Hallie asked, and though it was like she was trying to speak with bravado, I could hear the fear in her voice underneath. "Waiting until it would hurt me the most? Or are you just going directly to my school with the information?"

"No," I said, disappointed—but not surprised—that she would think only the worst of me. "I'm not going to do anything with it." Hallie let out a short laugh, and I pressed play on the footage again, suddenly remembering now exactly what Ford and I had been talking about. Sure enough, the conversation continued, playing out, my telling him I wanted us to hold on to it, and the look of relief on Ford's face the moment I said it. When we'd stopped talking, I pressed pause again and then turned to face Hallie. "See?"

"I just don't understand," she said after a moment, staring at the screen like it might provide some answers for her. "I mean . . . you could have really hurt me with this. Why didn't you?"

"I don't know," I said after a minute. I shrugged. "It felt like I would have been crossing a line I couldn't uncross. You know?"

Hallie looked at me for a moment and then nodded. I wondered if she was remembering the moment when she'd nearly framed me for theft—but then also pulled back at the last moment, leaving me fired from my job but without a criminal record. "Well . . . thank you," she finally said, and when she looked over at me, I could see the surprise—but also the gratitude—in her eyes. "I'm not going to use those scores," she said after a small pause. "I'm going to retake the test."

"You might want to tell Teddy," I said, surprising myself with the words even as I was saying them—and Hallie, too, judging by the expression on her face.

"*Teddy?*" she echoed incredulously. She just stared at me for a moment and then she went on. "We are talking about the same person, right? The guy with the unshakable moral compass? How do you really think this is going to go over with him? You have *met* Teddy, right?"

"I just think you're going to have to be honest with him—*totally* honest with him—if you guys are going to have a real shot," I said.

Hallie just looked at me for a second, and then she sighed and stared at the monitor again. I wasn't sure she was going to take my advice, but I could tell my words were getting through. "Maybe," she finally said in a small, quiet voice. But before I could reply, there was a ding, and a DVD slid out of the side of the monitor. "Looks like the footage is ready," she said. She gave me a nod. "Time for phase two."

Phase two involved actually getting Karen and my dad to see the video, and we'd come up with it on one of our many snack runs as we watched the group sitting on the couches, watching movies. We'd get this DVD into the player, invite Karen and my dad to join the group watching a movie, and then this—not one of Bruce's screeners—would come up. Both Hallie and I were planning on passing the blame on to Gwyneth, which would be made easier by the fact that she was currently in Los Angeles and not around to defend herself. But if things went according to plan, this would be the straw that broke the camel's back, what ended things with our parents once and for all. And it would hopefully be enough of a grenade tossed into the middle of their relationship that they wouldn't be stopping to ask questions, like where exactly the video had come from.

We'd now been lurking by the top of the steps for at least fifteen minutes, waiting for the group watching this latest movie to either take a break or finish watching. The break option was getting more likely, though, at least based on the amount of complaining I could hear about this particular movie (Josh had a problem with the screener's quality, and Reid was complaining about the subtitles, despite the fact that Sophie kept telling him they weren't subtitles, just antipiracy warnings).

After about five minutes of more complaining, they seemed to call it. Suddenly the sound cut off from the television, and I could hear the conversation sounds from the living room increase in volume. Hallie and I looked at each other, and then she started down the stairs first. I followed a few seconds later, holding the DVD.

I knew we probably wouldn't have that much time—just long enough for everyone to take a break and go grab snacks before regrouping. Luckily, when I went into the room, Hallie was standing by the television, but nobody else had returned yet. I nodded at her and crossed to the DVD player, ejecting the screener and sliding our disk into the player.

"Hey!" I straightened up and whirled around to see Sophie standing in the doorway of the living room, a bag of chips in her hand. "Where have you been? I haven't seen you all day. And you weren't helping the rest of us stack giant bags of sand in a hurricane."

"Right," I said, nodding, trying to think fast. While I'd told Sophie I was working with Hallie, I wasn't sure I should tell her about this latest plan—not only did I know she disapproved, but Hallie and I had discussed it, and we thought it would go over better if we were the only ones who knew what we were planning on showing everyone—that in addition to our parents being in the dark, it would sell it better if everyone else was too. "I've just been hanging out. You know, um . . . napping."

"Uh-huh," Sophie said. She nodded, but she kept her eyes on me, and I could see she knew there was more than I was saying. I looked away, breaking our eye contact. I'd tell her everything, once all this was over. Just not quite yet. She nodded at the TV. "Want to watch something?"

"Yeah," Hallie said, taking a step closer to me, her tone casual but her expression anything but. "Is the DVD ready to watch?"

"Um, almost," I said, looking at the front of the DVD player, which was still reading LOADING. Maybe because it was a DVD we'd burned ourselves, but this definitely seemed to be taking longer than usual. "I was thinking maybe we would see if my dad and Karen wanted to watch with us," I said, hoping my tone was just normal and not suspicious at all. "Maybe they're bored with writing and want a break."

"Great idea," Hallie said enthusiastically, giving me what was probably the world's least natural thumbs-up. "Should we call them? Or should someone go get them?"

Sophie folded her arms and looked at me, and I could tell she was trying to work out what exactly was going on. I heard a whirring sound and then looked down to see that the DVD player had stopped loading and was starting to play. I shot Hallie an excited look, and she nodded.

"Gemma," Sophie said, looking between me and Hallie, her frown deepening. "What's going—"

But she never finished her sentence, because at that moment, the power went out.

CHAPTER 14

I stood in the dark, my heart hammering, beyond glad for the moment that we were in blackness and nobody could see my face.

Because this was my fault.

There was nobody else to blame (well, other than the storm). But the current lack-of-power situation was all because of me—because no matter how many times Rosie had talked to me about it, and reminded me about it, I hadn't refilled the propane tanks. The generator had lost power—which meant the entire house had no power, not until the regular power came back on. And who knew how long that might take?

I blinked, waiting for my eyes to adjust, but it was *really* dark in the house. Even though it was still late afternoon, the fact was that the sun wasn't exactly shining outside. The black storm clouds covering the sky meant it was almost as dark outside as it would be at midnight—which meant it was now pitch-dark inside the mansion.

"What happened?" I heard someone ask—I was pretty sure it was Sophie.

"Looks like the generator's gone out," Hallie said from somewhere in the darkness.

"Looks like it," I said after a moment. After I spoke, I could feel my heart hammering, waiting for them to call me on this, to yell at me for not doing my job. But then, all at once, I remembered—Rosie had talked to just me on the phone. I knew Sophie wouldn't rat me out, and if I didn't own up to it, nobody had to know this was my fault. For just a moment, I convinced myself that this was the thing to do. But just as I'd decided this, the certainty faded.

Because it *was* my fault. And if I'd just done what I was supposed to do, and done it right, this wouldn't be happening now. I took a deep breath. "Actually—" I started, just as I heard a crash.

"What was that?" I heard Sophie ask just as Hallie yelped "Ow!" and I heard another, smaller crash.

I reached into my pocket for my phone but realized a moment too late it was up in the editing room—along with Hallie's. "Anyone have their phone on them?" I asked the room in general, since I didn't know who was currently in it.

"Yeah," I heard a voice say, and realized at some point Josh had joined us. "Hold on. I'll turn on the flashlight."

A second later Josh's phone illuminated, and I could see— not much, but something. Josh had crashed into the bookcase on his way into the room—there were books and knickknacks scattered by his feet—and Sophie and Hallie had crashed into each other, judging by the way they were both rubbing their heads. "What happened to the power?"

"The generator went out," Hallie said with a sigh.

"Uh-oh," Josh said softly, just as another clap of thunder sounded from outside, loud enough that it seemed to shake the very foundations of the house. I felt myself shiver. Somehow it had been easier to face the storm when there were at least lights we could turn on. Now, in the dark, looking at the rain lashing against the windows, it suddenly seemed much more ominous—and dangerous.

"Hello?" I heard a voice say, and I realized it was Teddy's.

"Hi," I called toward the sound of his voice. "Teddy—can you see the light? Come toward it."

Josh turned his phone toward the entrance of the living room, and I saw Teddy, walking slowly, his hands out in front of him. When he realized we could see him, he dropped his hands and stuck them in his pockets. "Hi," he said quietly to Hallie, who gave him a nod and then took a step away, crossing and uncrossing her arms, but not before I saw the look on her face—hurt, but trying very hard not to let it show.

"So the power's out," Sophie said to him as she carefully made her way across the room to sit on the couch.

"Well, the power had been out for a while," Hallie clarified. "Since yesterday?"

"Right," I said, wanting us to move past this topic of conversation as quickly as possible. "The generator had been on. But now that's out too."

The walkie on the coffee table suddenly came to life, static and my dad's voice cutting in and out. "Gemma?"

I made my way over to it cautiously and then pressed the button to talk. "Dad?"

"Our power's out over here," he said. "Are you guys okay?"

"Ours is out too," I said, then there was a slightly longer pause on his end. "Um, over and out," I said, wondering if maybe I wasn't using correct walkie language.

"Want us to come over there?" my dad asked. "Are you sure you're all right?"

I looked around. The problem with walkie-talkies was that having a private conversation—or just a conversation in which not everyone heard everything you were saying—was impossible. No wonder these things weren't going to be replacing cell phones anytime soon. "It's okay," I said as I realized it was okay. Now that the power was out, there was no point in getting my dad and Karen here—there was no footage for them to watch. And I had a feeling, because the guesthouse was so far away, that if they made the trek once, they wouldn't be doing it again, and would probably end up staying over here tonight. And that was something I didn't really want. If Hallie and I were going to be splitting them up, the less we saw them together and happy, the better.

"No, we're okay," I said into the walkie. "You guys stay dry. I'll let you know if there are any problems."

"Okay," my dad said after a moment, still sounding unsure but also a tiny bit relieved not to have to go walking through the storm. "But let me know if anything happens or if you need help. And we'll be there."

The *we* was enough to let me know I'd made the right call. "Sure," I said. "Will do." My dad said good-bye, and I set the walkie back down on the table. "So," I said, feeling like someone had to take charge. "It's just a power outage, guys. We can handle it."

"This just goes to show what I've been saying for ages," Teddy said, shaking his head. "We need to develop real alternate fuel sources. Otherwise, at some point, the power will go out . . . and won't *ever* come back on again."

"Um, okay," Josh said after a pause in which nobody seemed to know exactly what to say. "Good point. But for right now—"

"We need to get the candles and the flashlight," I said, listing them on my fingers. "This is why we got all that stuff ready, after all."

"Probably a good idea," Josh said as he glanced down at his phone screen. "I'm running low on battery power."

"You should probably turn the flashlight off then," Hallie said. "That drains the battery like crazy."

"Hallie's right," I said, even though I didn't exactly relish the idea of being thrown back into the darkness. "We need to keep our cell phones with some degree of charge in case we need to make an emergency call or something. Because right now, if they die, there's no way to charge them again."

Josh nodded and then pressed a button on his screen, and the living room went dark again. My eyes had adjusted some-what by now—I was no longer totally in darkness—but I could only make out vague shapes around me now; the features of the other people in the room had totally disappeared.

"I think the box of candles is still in the kitchen," I said, starting to move slowly in that direction. "I'll go get them."

"Want some help?" Sophie asked from the direction of the couch.

"No," I said, even though I really wouldn't have minded someone coming with me. Now that I was moving around in the dark on my own, I couldn't stop thinking about the noises Hallie and I had heard coming from the kitchen, and the flash of something I'd seen darting just out of frame in the security center. What if there really was a ghost—or, even worse, a mouse?

"You sure?" Hallie asked.

"Sure," I said, even though I really wasn't. But I knew it was probably best for everyone else to stay in once place, rather than having all of us fumbling around in the dark, knocking into things and each other. Having everyone accounted for and in one central location was probably the smartest thing we could do at the moment.

I started to walk slowly down the hall, one hand extended and touching the wall, just to give me a sense of where I was. As I shuffled my feet along, I was just hoping nobody had left anything lying around on the floor—I couldn't even see in front of my own hand, especially now, because there were no windows in the hallway. All it would take was an errant flip-flop for me to go sprawling.

When the hallway ended, I knew there was a room I had to cross before I made it into the kitchen. I had a vague sense of how far away it was, and I took a deep breath and started walking in that direction, hands extended out in front of me.

I was starting to relax a little when I felt myself bump into something. Not some*thing*, I realized a moment later—someone. "Oh—sorry," I said, starting to take a step back, but my feet got tangled, and I felt myself start to fall backward, off-balance.

"Careful," someone was saying, a strong hand reaching out and pulling me onto my feet, the other hand against my back. "You okay, Gem?"

It was Ford. "Yeah," I said, smiling in his direction. A moment later I realized how silly that was, since he couldn't see me—since neither of us could see *anything*. But I also realized I wasn't going to be able to stop. This was Ford. I was going to smile when he was near me; that was just the way these things worked.

"I was coming to look for you," he said. "I was worried."

"I think we're stuck in the dark until the power comes back on again," I said, wondering if I should tell him this was actually all my fault—if it would be easier to do it if I didn't have to look at him.

"I was headed for the candles in the kitchen," Ford said.

"That's where I was headed," I said. "Great minds think alike, and all that."

"I guess they do," Ford said, and even though I couldn't see him, I could hear the smile in his voice too.

All at once, I realized his hand was still on my back. I could practically feel the heat of it through my shirt and against my skin. I stretched my hand out in front of me and it collided with Ford's chest—he was right there, so close. This was closer than we'd ever been before. And even though we didn't have to stand this close—even though there was no *reason* for us to be standing this close—neither one of us was making any move to separate.

Ford moved his hand from the small of my back to my arm, going very slowly, never losing contact with me, moving millimeter by millimeter. He traced his fingers down my arm, and then they were brushing against mine, sending sparks zinging every place he touched me. I moved my other hand up from his chest until I found his face. I somehow couldn't believe I was doing this—couldn't believe this was happening right now.

I mean, this was *Ford*. And it was me. I had a feeling this was easier now that we could do this in the darkness, neither of us having to see the other, see all the history we had together, and worry we were doing the wrong thing, worry we were going to mess something up. Instead we could set all those fears aside for the moment, just be who we were in the darkness. And it felt *right*. That was the strangest thing of all, I realized—this didn't at all feel strange.

I stretched up and slowly, carefully ran my hand through his spiky black hair, just a little damp from his trip across from the pool house. Then I let my fingers trace down the curve of his cheek as Ford interlaced his fingers with mine, his thumb rubbing mine in a slow, lazy circle that gave me the shivers.

And even though I couldn't see that this was happening at all, I could somehow tell it was, as Ford tilted his head down toward mine as I stretched up toward him. We were so close, just a breath apart, and I could feel my heart beating so hard, I was sure the rest of the house could hear it too. Me and Ford—we were about to kiss, a second kiss that had been four years in the making.

"Hi," Ford said as I ran my hand over his jawline.

"Hi," I said back, closing my eyes, leaning toward him—

"Hi!" A new voice—a guy's voice—was suddenly much closer to me than I'd realized, and I froze and then jumped back, instinct taking over.

"Who is that?" I asked, looking around, my heart beating hard, but not in the excited about-to-kiss-the-guy-you-like way. More in the just-been-startled-by-a-strange-presence way. And one was definitely preferable to the other, I realized now.

"It's me," the voice said, sounding hurt he hadn't been recognized, even though you couldn't see *anything* in the hallway. After a moment I realized it was Reid—because who else would it have been, really? "What are you guys doing?"

"Nothing," Ford said after a moment, and I could hear the regret in his voice that this had turned out to be the case. He sounded exactly like I was currently feeling. "We weren't doing anything."

"I was just in the kitchen when all the lights went out," Reid went on pleasantly, apparently thinking we were all just going to stand around in the darkness, having this conversation. "Spooky, huh? Anyway. What's the plan now?"

"Do you have your phone with you?" I asked Reid, figuring Ford didn't have his with him, otherwise he would have used the flashlight by now.

"Yeah," Reid said, leading me to wonder why, in that case, he had been fumbling around in the dark and messing up other people's second kisses. "Want to call someone?"

"No," I said, biting back a sigh as Reid handed it to me by jabbing it into my arm. I turned on the flashlight feature, and when it illuminated, I could see Ford—and see just how close together we were still standing.

He was looking down into my eyes, and I worried he might look embarrassed, or like he was regretting he'd made a mistake—but there was nothing of the sort in his expression. He gave me that half-smile, one that seemed to say very clearly to me that we'd find another time. That this wasn't over yet.

"Okay," I said, making myself look away from Ford; otherwise, I was just going to give in and start kissing him, not even caring if Reid was right there. "Let's get some candles."

"We might need more than candles," Ford said as we all started to make our slow way toward the kitchen, an unlikely group of three. "If there's no TV, and people can't be on their computers and phones, we're going to need entertainment."

I smiled at him as we walked. "Did you have something in mind?"

<center>~~~~~~~~</center>

"No!" Hallie yelled as she rolled a five, and landed squarely on my property.

"Yep," I said, leaning back against the couch and smiling at her. "That's the way it goes. Pay up."

"I think you're cheating," Hallie grumbled as she looked around the coffee table in the flickering candlelight, clearly hoping for support. "Anyone else?"

"Think about what you say," I said, holding the bag of Doritos aloft, "for I am the keeper of the snacks." At that moment, though, Josh leaned over and plucked the bag from me. "Hey!" I yelped as he continued over to his couch with it. "I was making a point!"

"Oh, sorry," he said, reaching in and taking a handful. "I was hungry."

Ford laughed as Sophie gestured for Josh to give her the chips. Reid frowned, looking like he was a few beats behind, as usual.

It had been two hours since the power had gone out, and nobody was more surprised than me that we were all having . . . well, fun.

My dad had been checking up on us by walkie every half hour until I told him firmly we were *fine* and at this point we were only going to run the batteries down. He agreed to stop checking in, but only after I'd promised again to contact him, no matter what time it was, if we needed him. But when I'd signed off with him, I realized I was actually glad he was staying across the property for the night. It would be good to get some space, and not have to deal with my unhappy feelings toward him or to try to plot something to break up him and Karen. I could just *be*, which was a relief.

Ford had raided the board game collection in the pool house, and we'd returned to the living room with the one precious battery-powered flashlight, the box of *New Beginning* candles, and a stack of board games. We were working our way through them, and after this game of Monopoly, Hallie had promised to teach those of us who didn't know (me and Reid) how to play poker, and we were going to have a big game, everyone playing. Because everyone was here—well, except my dad and Karen.

We had all gathered in the living room—Me, Ford, Josh, Hallie, Sophie, Reid, and Teddy. And maybe because we didn't have any electronic devices to distract us, or because we couldn't watch a movie or TV, it was actually nice to hang out like this in a group. It also seemed like all the resentments and anger that had been flying around the day before had really dissipated, and we were now just able to have a good time. There was still some lingering tension between Hallie and Teddy, of course—they were sitting on separate couches and not speaking directly to each other if they both could avoid it—but aside from that, we were all getting along.

"You know, a monopoly is more than a game," Teddy said as he frowned down at his own meager pile of real-estate holdings. "Corporate monopolies are a major problem."

"I'm having a problem right now with Ford's monopolies." Sophie sighed as she looked at the board.

"Don't hate the player; hate the game," Ford said, and Josh laughed and held out his hand for a fist bump.

"Very nice," Josh said as Ford inclined his head modestly.

"Why, thank you," he said.

"I think we're done with board games," Hallie said as she put her own piece—the race car—down. "Who wants to play poker?"

"Is this just because you're losing?" I asked, raising an eyebrow at her.

"No," Hallie said, but even in the candlelight, I could see she was starting to blush. "I mean, no, I'm not."

"Yes, you actually are," Reid said helpfully as he looked at the board. "If you add up the amount of property, and the amount of debt . . ."

"Okay, fine," Hallie said as I laughed, and Sophie joined in. "But that doesn't mean it's still not poker time. Any takers?"

I took a breath to answer, but at that exact moment there was a loud crash from the kitchen.

"What was that?" Ford said, jumping to his feet.

"I don't know," I said, feeling my heart start to beat hard again, looking across the coffee table at Hallie. "Didn't that sound like what we heard the other night?"

"What was it?" Josh asked, also getting to his feet, his brow furrowed.

"We don't know," Hallie said. "We heard something in the kitchen, but there was nothing there by the time we arrived."

"Hallie said it was a mouse," I said, making myself laugh as I said it, like this was just so ridiculous and not at all something that terrified me.

"That wasn't a mouse," Ford said so definitively, I could feel myself start to relax.

"It wasn't?"

"A crash that big?" Ford shook his head. "More likely it was a rat."

"Oh my god," I muttered, pulling my legs up underneath me, suddenly feeling my skin crawl.

"Just because an animal isn't the cutest, doesn't mean it doesn't have its fundamental rights," Teddy said, shooting me a look. "It's actually called the Panda Paradigm, and—"

"Guys!" Josh said, and I looked over at him in surprise. "Fascinating as this is, I think we should go check it out."

"Yeah," Ford said, starting to head out toward the kitchen, switching on the flashlight as he went.

"I'll come too," I said, even though it was the last thing I wanted to do. But I also didn't want to be labeled as the person who was afraid of scary sounds in the dark—I knew if I stayed, Ford might not let me live it down.

"Me too," Sophie said, shooting me a look. I could see from her expression that she knew just how freaked out I was and was coming along for support. Sophie was totally fearless when it came to crawling furry things—but she was afraid of clowns for some reason, so it all balanced out.

The four of us headed down the hall to the kitchen, Ford leading the way with the flashlight. "I actually don't think there's going to be anything there," Ford said. To Josh and Sophie, he probably came across as totally confident, but I could hear the slight hesitation in his voice, and I knew there was a piece of him that was worried about what we were going to find. "People's breakfast dishes got knocked over, the wind shook something loose, something like that. Or maybe Paul or Karen came in looking for a snack or something. There's going to be a logical explanation. Trust me. It's—"

But whatever he was about to say next was lost, as his flash-light beam swept across the kitchen, to the open fridge door and the person standing behind it. We all drew in a collective breath as the door swung closed and Gwyneth Davidson stood there, looking only slightly embarrassed as she held up her hand to block the flashlight beam.

"Oh hey," she said, giving us a wave. "What's up, guys?"

CHAPTER 15

"Explain this to me again," Hallie said, her tone incredulous. "You've been here this *whole time*?"

Gwyneth tossed her hair over her shoulder as she crossed her legs on the couch. A mini-tribunal had sprung up in the living room, Gwyneth sitting on the couch as we stood around her, most of us trying to get answers, everyone talking all at once, which wasn't moving us very far along in terms of the answer-getting. "Kind of," she finally said.

"Wait a second," Ford said, shaking his head as he sat next to his sister. "Why have you been hiding in your own house?"

"Yeah," Sophie piped up, raising her eyebrows. "Why tell us all you were in L.A. when you've been here from the beginning?"

"Wait, she's been here from the beginning?" Reid asked, his brow knitting in confusion.

"I should have known," I said, shaking my head, all the pieces falling into place just a little too late. I looked over at Ford.

"Remember? It was the same thing she pulled the night of the SuperChef dinner. She was hiding in Bruce's office the whole time."

"Look," Gwyneth said loudly, and everyone else quieted down. "Everyone seemed really mad about the whole video thing at Hallie's party. So I thought it might be better not to have to deal with that kind of energy. I tried to go back to L.A., but no flights were getting out. So I figured the next best thing was letting you *think* I'd headed out of town."

"It was you we kept hearing in the kitchen," I said, finally putting this together, just a day too late. I said a silent apology to Teddy.

"And did you eat all the cereal?" Ford asked, suddenly sounding more angry about this than he had about anything else so far.

"It's not easy," Gwyneth snapped. "I had to get food when nobody would be around. I'm staying in some godforsaken room in the east wing. . . ."

"Hey!" Reid said, brightening. "I knew it. Didn't I tell you guys I heard a TV on in there?"

"You did," I said, nodding, suddenly feeling bad for dismissing his claims so easily. "Um, sorry about that, Reid."

"And then I heard you two messing around in my editing room," she said, turning to face me and Hallie. "I hope you didn't do any damage." Everyone turned to look at me and Hallie as we both suddenly became very interested in the floor.

"What were you doing in there?" Sophie asked, sounding baffled.

"Um," Hallie said, looking at me, and I knew without her even having to say anything that she was blanking and wanted me to jump in.

"We just needed a spot to talk," I said after a moment. Sophie looked at me evenly, and I could tell she didn't quite believe this story.

"Well," Gwyneth said, and huffed, seeming to forget she was the one in trouble here. "Everything better be just as I left it."

"Why?" Ford asked, sharpness in his voice. "You didn't want them to see how you'd manipulated things for your benefit?"

"Oh, come *on*," Gwyneth said, rolling her eyes. "Every documentarian does it. And it's not like you guys are so special. I was doing it even when I thought it was going to be about Bruce."

"You were?" I asked, baffled, since I'd been here then and didn't remember anything.

"Um, yeah," Gwyneth said, like all this was just to be expected. "I sent a friend here pretending to be a reporter, wanting to get a picture of Bruce's stupid Spotlight award. I hadn't realized you'd gotten it fixed. I was hoping to have the pot stirred a little, and tensions running high, before people put the cameras on. But no such luck."

I looked across at Hallie, and felt my jaw fall. So it hadn't been her behind it. All this time, I'd been convinced it had been Hallie, promising me on the beach she was done and then not even an hour later sending in someone to get me in trouble with Bruce. I'd just assumed she was lying and couldn't be trusted. It was the reason I'd doubled down and gone with Sophie to steal Hallie's job. To which she, of course, had retaliated in turn . . .

It had been the beginning of our whole revenge war. And it had been based on a mistake.

"So you were telling the truth," I said slowly, turning to look at Hallie. "When you told me you were done."

"I was," she said, nodding, and I wondered if she was feeling the same thing I was—like maybe everything we'd put each other through over the last few weeks could have been avoided.

"Oh," I said, nodding. "Um . . ." I looked over at her. An apology was on the tip of my tongue, but I hesitated. I'd only reacted as I had because of what she'd put me through the month before. And it wasn't like either of us had pulled our punches when we'd been caught up in it, both of us escalating until I didn't recognize myself any longer. I realized I was sorry—but mostly, I was sorry we'd both had to go through that, when it was kicked off by a misunderstanding that could have been avoided.

"Yeah," Hallie said, and I now knew from her expression she was feeling pretty much the same way I was.

"I just don't know why you didn't just tell us you were here," Ford said, shaking his head, and bringing me back to the present moment—Gwyneth and the fact that she'd been here all along.

"Uh, because all of you were really mad at me," Gwyneth said, like this was the most obvious thing in the world. "Why would I want to deal with that?"

"Because it would have been the right thing to do," I said, without even realizing I was going to. Ford and Gwyneth started arguing again, about the cereal he was now insisting she replace, but I wasn't really paying attention. For me it was like I kept hearing my own words reverberating in my head. I had been really annoyed to find out Gwyneth had been here, hiding rather than facing the music. But it wasn't until this moment I realized why that was.

I understood now, the realization crashing in on me, inescapable and true. It was because Gwyneth wasn't the only person in this room who ran and hid from things when they got to be too much. That was what I did too. Whether it was running away and not fixing the mess I'd made with Karen and Hallie when I was eleven, or not having the courage to tell my dad about what was happening in my life—either five years ago or this summer, or tonight—or not admitting to the power outage being my fault. I just avoided and dodged and hoped for the best. But the best never seemed to come—the truth always came out, one way or another, and by that point people were much angrier with you than they would have been if you had just owned up from the beginning.

This was Gwyneth's mode of operating—but that didn't mean I wanted it to be mine. Seeing it in front of me made me realize that wasn't what I wanted to do. Not anymore.

"I should actually say something," I piped up. Everyone was still talking among themselves, nobody paying any attention to me, and I realized I'd have to try again, as tempting as it was to just say I'd tried but nobody had paid attention and so I'd had to give up. I took a big breath and then yelled, "Hey!"

Everyone turned to look at me now, the conversations that had been going on now abandoned. "Uh, you okay, Gem?" Ford asked, raising an eyebrow at me.

"Yeah," I said. And then, before I could talk myself out of it, or wonder if I should be saying this, I went on, "I need to confess something to you guys. The power's out because of me. I was supposed to refill the propane tanks, and I didn't." Everyone was still looking at me, and I noticed, my heart starting to beat a little harder, that nobody looked very happy. "Um, sorry."

"So are we done here?" Gwyneth asked, maybe seeing this as her opportunity for escape as she stood up, covering a yawn with one hand. "Because I'd really like to get some sleep."

"No." The voice came from the back of the room, and I saw it was Josh who'd spoken. His voice was quiet but it carried, and as Gwyneth looked at him, some of her bravado seemed to slip away a little. It was like she'd forgotten, until this moment, that she'd left her boyfriend hanging this whole time and now had to face the consequences of that.

"Oh right," Gwyneth said, her voice much quieter now. "Um, hi, Josh. What's up?"

"I think we should talk, don't you?" he asked. It was a question that really didn't need an answer, and Gwyneth seemed to realize this. She nodded and then grabbed the one flashlight off the coffee table as they headed out of the living room, not walking too close together.

"Yikes," Sophie murmured when they were out of earshot.

"Yeah," Hallie said. "I don't see that ending well."

"Wait," I said, looking around, surprised everyone had already moved on so quickly. "You guys aren't mad at me?"

"I'd be more mad if you'd caused the power to go out in the

first place," Ford said as he passed me on his way to the couch. "But the generator wasn't going to be able to get us back online, so I really don't have a stake in this."

"And I thought tonight was really kind of fun," Reid said quietly, surprising me. "So I didn't mind having no power."

"Oh," I said as that all sunk in. I'd somehow expected my confession might not be taken this well, and even though it had felt good to say it, this was actually a little bit anticlimactic.

"We *could* be mad at you if you want us to be," Hallie said after a pause.

"No, I'm good," I said immediately. "Thanks, though."

"I think it's actually been an illuminating metaphor," Teddy said, gesturing big with his hands, seeming to indicate the entire room. I inwardly groaned. Whenever Teddy started talking about "illuminating metaphors," I would invariably try not to fall asleep while standing up.

"It is?" Sophie asked, sounding baffled.

"Indeed," Teddy said, clearly warming to his theme as I shot Sophie a look. She'd known Teddy for two years now; I would have thought she would have remembered never to engage with him when he started talking about interesting metaphors. "Because there's a larger energy crisis afoot, and nobody wants to take the blame for that, either. But in the end—"

"Hey." I looked over to see Gwyneth coming back into the living room, the flashlight beam sweeping across all of us. I looked around her to see if Josh was coming back with her, but she seemed to be alone. "So Josh and I broke up," she said matter-of-factly. I wasn't really that shocked by this—I would have been much more surprised if they had somehow found a way to stay together, after the video and after Gwyneth pretending to leave town. But even so, out of the corner of my eye, I saw Sophie hand Hallie a dollar. I just hoped Gwyneth hadn't seen— even if the breakup was mutual, it was still not the best thing to learn that people had placed wagers on it.

"Oh," Reid said sympathetically. "I'm sorry to hear that. What happened?"

Gwyneth just shot him a look, and it was clear she had no intention of answering the question. "Someone get him up to speed for me?" she asked as she turned the flashlight beam off and set it back down on the table. She yawned again, covering her mouth with her hand. "I'm going to bed."

"Wait, where's my brother?" Hallie asked, looking around.

Gwyneth shrugged. "I don't know. He said he needed some 'alone time,'" she said, putting air quotes around the last two words.

I looked at the flashlight on the table and realized it was our last one. "Wait, so you just left him in the dark?"

"No," Gwyneth said with an exasperated sigh. I was getting the distinct sense from her that Josh wasn't the only one currently in need of some alone time. "I explained everything carefully." I felt myself frown, and then Gwyneth glanced at the flashlight and smiled. "Oh, *literally* in the dark. Well, yeah, I guess so. But he'll be fine. I'll see you guys tomorrow!" she called over her shoulder as she started heading up the steps toward her room.

"My sister's a little . . ." Ford looked after her and shook his head. "I'm going to have a word with her," he said. He shot me a quick smile. "Be right back."

I looked at the flashlight on the table again. I was suddenly remembering how it had felt when Teddy had all of a sudden ended things in the Target gardening aisle. I couldn't do anything to make it better—but I could at least bring Josh a flashlight. "I'm going to give this to him," I said, picking it up off the table and turning it on. "I'll be right back."

CHAPTER 16

"Josh?" I called as I pointed the flashlight beam down the hall. With all the candles and all the people gathered in the living room, it really did seem a lot brighter than the rest of the house. Walking around it now, I was really noticing just how dark it was. It was pitch-black, and almost totally silent, except for the roar of the wind and the sound of the rain beating down on the roof. Though since that had been going on continually for two days now, it was just starting to fade into background noise. It was also incredibly spooky, the flashlight creating shadows that seemed huge against the walls of the mansion. If Gwyneth hadn't been revealed as the potential ghost (or mouse), I wasn't sure I would have been able to do this by myself. Even now I was trying not to jump at every sound I heard, every shadow that seemed somehow ominous. I was getting freaked out enough, and I was the one with the flash-light. It was making me feel, with every step I took, that I'd done the right thing in going to look for Josh. It was all well and good to want to be alone right after a breakup. It was another whole thing to then have to find your way back in a pitch-black house.

I had a feeling Josh had stayed downstairs—and it didn't seem like he and Gwyneth had gone very far. But even so, I was now regretting I hadn't asked her for more concrete information before she'd gone to bed. "Josh?" I called again, sweeping my beam across the foyer, and as I did, trying to tell myself there was nothing scary at all about a giant life-size stuffed polar bear.

"Gemma?" The voice was behind me, and even though I'd told myself I was ready for this, I still jumped.

I turned around, my heart pounding, to see Josh sitting on the floor in the foyer, facing the front doors. "What are you doing here?" I asked, looking around. Of all the places I had been looking for him, this had not been the place I'd expected to find him. For one thing, the marble floor was really hard and not that comfortable to sit on. And for another, the polar bear was looking *really* spooky in the intermittent lightning flashes. I couldn't be the only one who thought so.

"Thought about leaving," he said with a shrug and a sigh. "But when I got here, I realized just how stupid that was."

"It's not stupid," I said, crossing over toward him. I suddenly remembered what I hadn't let myself think about in months—how, after Teddy had broken my heart, I hadn't been able to face riding back home with him in his Prius, and had to call Walter to pick me up. He'd arrived wearing full waders and had talked to me about trout the whole drive home and it had been horrible. So I understood the impulse—you sometimes needed a moment to yourself, just to process everything that had happened. Which was harder if you were currently staying in the same house with the person who'd just broken up with you. "I get it."

"What are you doing here?" he asked.

After hesitating for just a moment, I came and sat down next to him, placing the flashlight on the floor between us.

"Didn't want you to be stuck in the dark," I said, gesturing to the flashlight.

Josh gave me a small smile. "Thanks," he said with a nod. "That's really nice of you."

"Gwyneth told us what happened," I said after a moment, and Josh nodded.

"Yeah," he said with a sigh. "I haven't really had the best luck romantically this summer."

"It's not over yet," I said, trying to look on the bright side, as Josh shook his head. "I mean . . . at least her name actually *was* Gwyneth. So that's an improvement."

Josh let out a short laugh. "That's a good point," he said, raising an eyebrow at me. "I hadn't thought of it that way."

Silence fell between us for a moment, and Josh picked up the flashlight and rolled it between his palms, scattering light around the room.

"Are you okay?" I asked.

Josh set the flashlight down. "I am," he said, like he was realizing this as he said it. "I will be." He looked over at me, his eyes searching mine for a moment. "Are we okay?" he asked slowly.

I looked back at him. Only a few weeks ago I would have wondered what this meant . . . if it meant there was a future with us. Where it would lead us romantically, and if we would have another chance. But as I looked at him now, I realized all that tension was totally gone. There were no more sparks flying between us, no more longing glances or unspoken words. It was just . . . comfortable. Like you would be around an old friend.

I suddenly thought of the passage I'd read in the book of Bruce's ex-wife, the one who'd wanted to be a florist. About the *almost* bloom. The one that never quite turned out, never quite achieved its full potential, but shouldn't have been thrown away or discounted because of that. Maybe, I realized as I looked over at him now, that was what Josh and I were. We were nothing but potential that, in the end, went unrealized. Maybe we'd missed our window; maybe it never would have worked out. But we'd never actually know . . . and I realized I was fine with that.

"We're good," I said, hoping my voice sounded as definitive as I felt. "What do you think?" I asked, giving him a small smile. "Friends?"

Josh looked at me for a moment and then gave me a half-smile of his own. "Friends," he echoed, a slight question in his tone. If he was disappointed, if he would have chosen a different path, I didn't know. But I knew it didn't matter. This was where we were supposed to end up, at long last. Josh slung an arm around my shoulders and gave me a quick kiss on the forehead. "Sounds good," he said. I dropped my head onto his shoulder for just a second. There was nothing romantic in it—it just felt comforting. I was starting to move away when I heard something crash to the ground behind us.

Josh and I broke apart, and I looked over to see Ford, his phone in pieces on the ground in front of him, his expression beyond hurt.

"Ford," I said, scrambling to my feet. I could only imagine how that must have looked, especially without any real light to see what was happening. I took a step closer to him, but Ford was already turning and running out, not looking behind him, not stopping even as I yelled out his name.

CHAPTER 17

"**F**ord?" Sophie asked as she reluctantly looked away from Reid. I'd yelled after Ford until I'd realized he wasn't coming back, and then I'd started to run after him, before I remembered we were in a pitch-black mansion, and the last thing I wanted to do was to go wandering around alone in the dark. So Josh and I had hurried back to the living room, where Sophie and Reid were the only ones still awake—apparently, Hallie had gone to bed, and Teddy had gone back to meditate and journal on the day by candlelight. Josh headed up to bed shortly after that, and now that I was here with just Sophie and Reid, it was clear they had been enjoying some alone time—nobody sat that close to each other on a couch unless they had been or would be making out. Even in my current state, I made a mental note to ask her about it as soon as we had some time alone. Although judging by Reid's smitten expression, I probably could have asked her in front of him, and he really wouldn't have cared all that much.

"He was here," Reid piped up. "He looked upset about something. Everything okay?"

I practically had to bite my lip to keep from screaming. It wasn't Reid's fault, really, and he didn't deserve that. But I needed answers, and I needed them now. "No," I said, my voice serious enough that Sophie's head snapped up—it was like she finally saw what was going on with me.

"Gem, what is it?" she asked, her brow furrowed.

"I just need to speak to him," I said, looking around the room. I didn't want to wait until the morning, letting Ford spend the night thinking he'd just seen me and Josh being romantic, when the fact was, the exact opposite was true. I needed to tell Ford how I felt about *him*. I'd needed to tell him for a while now, and I was kicking myself that I hadn't done it before. If I'd done it before, this wouldn't be happening now. If I'd just gotten up the courage to tell him, not waited for the perfect moment or proof he might feel the same way, all this confusion would have been resolved. "I'm going to go check the pool house."

"He's probably there," Sophie said with a nod as she cuddled back up to Reid. "Also, let me know if he got the Internet working again. It sounded like it."

"What do you mean?" I asked, even though a piece of me was screaming at myself not to ask, just to go find Ford and deal with the Internet later on, to get my priorities straight.

"Just because he said something about surfing," Sophie said with a shrug, and I felt myself, all of a sudden, go very cold. It felt like my heart had just plunged into my stomach.

"He said that?" I asked faintly. "He said he was going surfing?"

"Something like that," Reid said with a nod. He shot me a sheepish grin. "I'm afraid we were a little . . . distracted."

I looked out in the direction of the water, feeling my heart beat twice as hard as usual. I knew somehow Ford hadn't been talking about the Internet. It seemed like in whatever he thought he'd seen happening with me and Josh, it had made him forget his promise to me—and he'd gone surfing. "Gotta go," I said, grabbing the flashlight and taking it with me as I ran toward the kitchen.

"Gem?" I heard Sophie call out after me, but I didn't stop, didn't even hesitate. I started to run right out the doors that would lead me down past the pool house and toward the water when something propped in the corner of the kitchen caught my eye. It was the white life jacket from the boat, the one I'd taken with me as we'd disembarked.

Feeling like maybe a life jacket wouldn't be the worst idea in the world, I pulled it on and tightened the strap around me as I yanked open the door and was immediately hit with a blast of wind and rain.

I'd been avoiding the outside as much as possible, and so I hadn't realized just how bad it had gotten until I stood out in it, being lashed by the rain and trying to get my bearings. Even with the flashlight beam, I could barely see in front of me, though the occasional flashes of lightning gave me some visibility. But now that I was actually standing outside in the storm, they were more terrifying than comforting, because I was suddenly racking my brain to try to remember what to do if you were caught outside during a lightning storm. Were you supposed to go for open ground or avoid open ground? The only thing I could seem to remember at the moment was to not hold a gold club or a kite with a key on the end, neither of which were facts that were very helpful at the moment.

I aimed the flashlight beam around, praying Ford would be sitting on one of the lounge chairs or something, having realized going surfing in this weather was a terrible, stupid idea. But no such luck. The area was empty, the rain pelting down into the pool, the wind causing mini-waves to appear on the normally placid surface.

"Ford!" I screamed, even though the wind seemed to pick up my words and carry them away the second I opened my mouth. Of course, there was no answer—but I hadn't really expected there would be. I took a breath, trying not to notice how much I was already shivering, how my clothes were already soaked through and plastered to me.

I started to make my way down to the water, telling myself with every step that I'd see him sitting on the beach, that he hadn't *really* gone surfing in this, that he wouldn't have done that to me. The rain was bad enough, but it was the wind I was unprepared for. It felt like I was in danger of being picked up and tossed off my feet, or at the very least knocked over by a flying branch or tree—or a small car, since this wind felt strong enough to pick any of those up.

I made it down to the water's edge and felt my jaw drop. The ocean was huge, and like I'd never seen it before. The waves seemed angry, crashing down with a force that left me shaking. I'd always felt the ocean at night was scary enough and had never liked it when Ford had gone out night surfing. But I would have taken that any day over this. Because this was beyond terrifying. It was like something out of a nightmare.

"Ford!" I yelled, feeling increasingly frantic as I passed my flashlight beam over the sand, then over the water, where it was instantly swallowed by the blackness of the ocean. I moved it back to the sand—which was when I saw the surfboard.

I ran up to it, brushing droplets off my face. It was Ford's surfboard. He'd once shown me that he'd had it specially made so he could go night surfing. Why was it lying on the sand? What did that mean?

I didn't want to let myself think this through to the end—I wouldn't let myself. Without giving it a second thought, I dropped my flashlight, kicked off my flip-flops, grabbed the board, and ran toward the waves.

The cold of the water hit me like a shock, and I couldn't help but wish I'd taken Ford up on any of his many, many offers to teach me to surf over the years—offers that had taken place in the daytime, when there wasn't a hurricane, when I wasn't panicked something had happened to one of the people I cared about most in the world. As I clung to the board, struggling to keep my head above water as I tried frantically to see him, it occurred to me that maybe I should have called someone—the coast guard, or the Navy, or someone. But I also knew I wouldn't have been able to stop myself. Ford was in danger, which meant I had to run toward that danger, even if I had no idea what I was doing.

I tried to paddle out against the waves, the muscles in my arms already burning. I pushed my hair, which was plastered down against my face, out of my eyes. I was beyond grateful for my life vest, which was at least helping me to stay afloat, even though it was making it that much harder to hang on to my board. "Fo—" I started to yell, just as a giant wave crashed down over me.

I was tossed about, pulled into the wave's undertow. My life jacket brought me up to the surface, sputtering, and I gripped the surfboard as hard as I could, even as I felt it slipping out of my hands. "No," I said, coughing, as I watched it be swept away by a truly giant wave, then holding my breath as it crested over me, just praying it wouldn't be flung down onto my head.

When I surfaced again, I swam in a circle. Looking for shore, but it was just blackness and water and rain and wind, and I couldn't get my bearings. And I didn't see Ford anywhere, and what did that mean? "Ford!" I yelled, coughing and crying, the rain mixing with the tears of panic and exhaustion and fear I wasn't able to keep in any longer.

Just then a strong hand reached down and grabbed me by my waist, and I was being pulled up—onto a surfboard. I turned and saw Ford behind me, in a wetsuit, looking furious. "What are you *doing*?" he yelled over the sound of the wind and the crashing waves.

"I'm saving you!" I coughed, just trying to get my breath back. "Are you okay?"

"You can't wear this," Ford said, as he unbuckled my life jacket and pulled it over my head. "It's dangerous!"

"I lost your board," I said, looking around for it. I could feel myself start to shake; my teeth were beginning to chatter, and I wasn't sure I'd ever been quite this cold.

"I don't care," Ford said, looking back behind us at the waves. "I have to get you out of this. Can you hang on?"

I nodded, and Ford started paddling. He glanced behind him and drew in a breath, and even though I didn't want to, I looked as well and felt my heart drop when I saw the size of the wave coming for us. "Ford," I whispered.

"Hold on!" he yelled, and I pulled my knees up and gripped the board as hard as I could. "I'm going to try to get us through this—" he started, but the rest of his sentence was lost as the wave came down on us. Ford was holding on to me and holding on to the board and we were flying through the waves and the board was rocking from side to side and it was like we were in the middle of a washing machine and I couldn't tell what side was up and where I was until suddenly we were out of the water and Ford was grabbing me by the hand and pulling the board out from underneath me, yelling something I couldn't understand.

"What?" I yelled as I turned around, trying to get my bearings.

"Shore!" Ford yelled, already tugging me in the direction of it. It was so dark, and so rainy, it almost looked the same as the ocean. But I trusted Ford, and stumble-swam until my feet were firmly on the ground. I started to stop at the edge of the water, but Ford kept going, moving up with me until we were halfway to Bruce's before he dropped his surfboard and turned to me. "What were you doing out there?" he yelled above the sound of the wind and the crashing waves. "You could have been killed!"

"I was worried about you!" I yelled back at him. Now, looking at him on dry land, it only just began to hit me that he was okay, and the relief of it made my legs feel wobbly. "I saw your surfboard, and I thought something had happened to you."

"Gemma," Ford said, shaking his head. Rain was pouring down his face, which was a mask of utter confusion, like what I'd done was beyond his understanding. "It's a hurricane! You don't know how to surf! Why in the world would you have risked that?"

I looked at him through the rain, at the face that was so dear to me, and knew I would have done it again, without any hesitation, if it meant I could have brought him to safety. I realized a moment later I knew just how to answer his question—there was, in fact, only one answer.

And so I took a step closer to him and leaned forward, into the rain, and kissed him.

CHAPTER 18

I opened my eyes slowly and yawned. The first thing I noticed was that something was missing. It took me a moment to realize what it was, and a second later it hit me. The sound of rain was gone. It was very quiet, except for the occasional sounds of birds chirping. The light streaming into the pool house was bright—not bright enough that I'd need sunglasses, but after the near darkness of the last two days, it was a welcome change. It was over, I realized, as I took it in, the lack of rain that had been our constant soundtrack. The storm had broken.

"Hey," Ford said from behind me, tightening his arms around me.

I felt myself smile, my heart beating hard. "Hey, yourself," I said, threading one of my hands through his, still not quite able to believe I could do this.

We'd slept in the pool house together—but just slept, nothing had happened—well, unless you count some of the best kisses

I'd ever gotten in my life. But after we'd gotten out of the rain and we'd both changed into dry clothes (Ford had lent me sweat pants and a T-shirt with an equation on it), we'd kissed for a while, and it had been *wonderful*—but we'd both been wiped out from our hurricane surfing. Ford had offered to stay on the couch, but I had wanted to stay close to him for as long as possible, and we'd ended up falling asleep like big and little spoons, his arms around me like he was never going to let me go.

"Is the power back on?" he asked around a yawn, and I squinted at the digital clock on his bedside table. But the numbers weren't flashing the random time it had been when the power had gone out. The screen was just black and dead.

"Sorry," I said, turning back to him. "Not yet. Still no Internet."

"You know," Ford said, sounding shocked by this as he kissed my shoulder, and then the spot where my shoulder met my neck, and then my neck, making me shiver. "It seems like I don't actually mind all that much."

"Really," I said, turning to him, feeling a smile tugging at the corner of my lips. "You don't say." I had just leaned in for a kiss when Ford's phone beeped.

He groaned and reached for it, pulling on his glasses as he did. "I don't even recognize this number," he grumbled as he stared at his screen. "What are they doing, interrupting us?"

I turned to read it and saw I did know the number—it was Sophie.

Sophie Curtis

Hey! You okay? We're looking for you.
Your dad's starting to get worried—stalling as long as I can, but maybe get over here? Like, now?

I groaned even as I sat up. I knew that unless I wanted my dad to make his way out to the pool house and find me and Ford in bed together, I should get moving. I really didn't want to have to explain to my dad that nothing had happened, even though nothing had. Except some kissing. (Which I also didn't think my dad needed to know about.)

"What?" Ford asked. I handed him the phone, and his eyes widened as he read the message. "Uh-oh," he said.

"Yeah," I said, pushing myself out of bed and trying to smooth down my hair. I looked at what I was wearing and just hoped my dad wouldn't notice I was wearing clothes that were so obviously Ford's. "I'm going to go let them know I'm okay."

"And then you'll come back here," Ford said, his tone matter-of-fact.

I felt myself smile. There was a piece of me that still couldn't quite believe this was happening; still couldn't quite believe the two of us had ended up here. I kept waiting for it to seem strange or weird or awkward, but it didn't. It just felt *right*, like this was what we were supposed to be doing, like this was the way things had always been meant to be. "Of course," I said, leaning over and giving him a quick kiss.

Well, I'd *intended* for it to be a quick kiss. At least five minutes—maybe ten—passed before we came to our senses. I extricated myself and then ran across the pool deck to the main house, avoiding the tree branches scattered every few feet. Now that it was clear, you could really see just how destructive the storm had been. I let out a breath as I pulled open the sliding glass doors and headed inside, beyond grateful we'd all escaped the storm without any real damage.

The kitchen was empty, so I made my way toward the living room, just happy to be able to do this without needing flashlights or candles.

"Gem?" I turned around and saw Sophie running toward me, her eyes widening when she saw me. "Oh my god," she squealed. "Are you *kidding* me? You have to tell me everything!"

"Tell you what?" Hallie asked, coming to join us. I noticed she was carrying the dress she'd worn at the party over her arm, and holding her party shoes in her hand. Hallie looked at my outfit and raised an eyebrow at me. "It looks like you had a nice night."

"Shut up," I said, feeling my face get hot. I nodded at the dress and shoes. "Going somewhere?"

Hallie nodded and then headed toward the living room, Sophie and I following behind. "My mom got a call from her car service this morning—the roads have opened up, so they're *finally* on their way."

"Oh," I said, nodding. It was ridiculous to be sad about this— there had been far too many people and far too much drama in the house. But the truth was, I was a little disappointed. I finally understood what Reid had been getting at the night before.

Despite everything else—or maybe because of it—it had been fun.

It was clear now, though, that the fun was over. Josh was standing near the door, and Reid was standing next to him, both of them dressed in the suits they'd worn to the party, which by now looked wrinkled and rumpled. Teddy was standing a little awkwardly next to them, and I wondered if maybe he was getting a ride with Karen, or if he was just going back to Connecticut on the Jitney like he'd planned. Either way, at least from his proximity to the door, it seemed that he was ready to leave the house. Gwyneth was nowhere to be seen, but I wasn't really surprised. I had a feeling she'd show up around noon, when she was absolutely sure the house was free of the unexpected guests who'd descended.

"We made it," Hallie said, shaking her head.

"I know," I said, matching the disbelief in her tone. All of us together, under one roof, in a hurricane . . . I was amazed the house, and all of us, were still standing.

"I'm just going to say good-bye to Reid," Sophie said as she shot me a significant look. "And then we are going to *talk*."

I laughed at the fierceness in her expression. "Sounds good," I said, realizing I had to get all the details on how she and Reid had gotten together as well. Suddenly sitting down with my best friend—and only her, not eight other people—was sounding amazing.

Sophie ran across the room to Reid like they'd been separated for hours, and not a few minutes, and I turned back to Hallie, who was smoothing down the dress over her arm. "So,"

Hallie said after a moment of silence, giving me a tiny smile. "This was unexpected," she said.

"I know," I said. I suddenly flashed back to two days earlier, when Hallie and I had been in here, screaming at each other. It felt like much longer than that, somehow. And it wasn't like we were best friends, but . . . I thought back to our time in the editing suite and, despite my worries, how much fun it had been to be on the same side with her again, the two of us working on a project. It had taken me by surprise, but for just a moment . . . it had been like we'd been friends again. Like maybe we'd never stopped.

"I guess I'll see you around?" she asked, just as my dad and Karen came into the room, holding hands.

"Morning, all," Karen said, smiling at us and dropping my dad's hand to give Hallie a one-armed hug.

"Do we have everyone accounted for?" my dad asked in his joking voice. "We didn't lose anyone, did we?"

"Nope," I said a bit too heartily, resolving then and there to never tell him about my midnight dip in the ocean. There were just some things he didn't need to know, and it would only upset him. "But we did add someone. Gwyneth's here."

"Oh," my dad said. His brow furrowed, and I could tell he was trying to work out just how that had happened.

"I'll explain later," I said, and he nodded.

"Thank you so much for putting us all up," Karen was saying as she glanced at her phone. "The driver should be here any minute, but I just wanted to take a moment to—" The rest of Karen's sentence was lost as, all at once, noise started coming from every part of the house—beeping and clicking and whir-ring. Suddenly all the overhead lights and table lamps were on, and it was much brighter in the room than it had been only a moment before.

"Power's back on," Reid said helpfully, just in case any of us might have missed this.

"Ford will be happy," I said to Hallie, who was pulling out her phone.

"*I'm* happy," she said. "Now I can finally turn this thing back on. I've been afraid to in case it died."

"I know," I said, looking around for my own phone and then realizing I'd left it upstairs. "It's been—"

"What is that?" It was my dad who'd asked the question, his voice sharp. I looked over to see what he was looking at, and I felt my stomach plunge.

The TV had turned on, and with it, the DVD player as well. And the video Hallie and I had made was starting to play at full volume on Bruce's big screen. "Is that me?" he asked.

Karen gave a little laugh, taking a step closer to the TV and smoothing down her hair. "What is this?"

"Um," I said as I looked at Hallie frantically, and saw the same look of panic in her eyes. This was what we'd wanted, right? For our parents to see this? So why did I want to just turn it off and pretend this had been a mistake?

"Must be Gwyneth's documentary," my dad was saying as he squinted at the TV. "It's for a—" But then there was a quick cut, and the real footage started playing. There was my dad at the kitchen counter, talking to Rosie. "*It's a crime against literature,*" he was saying, going to on describe just how awful Karen's book was.

"What?" Karen whispered, going pale. She looked at my dad, and the shock mixed with sadness on her face was so painful, I had to look away from it.

The video changed again, and now my dad was sitting in the office, talking with Bruce. *"I think this writer actually thinks this is good,"* he was saying as Bruce laughed. *"Are we sure this isn't just some joke on the part of the publishing industry?"*

I looked at Hallie, who cast a stricken look back at me, as on and on the video played, seeming much longer than it had been when we'd been putting it together in the editing suite. I felt sick by the time it finally ended, and the screen went black. Karen was crying quietly. My dad's face was pale, and he was holding on to the back of the couch for support, looking like someone who had no idea what had just happened to him.

"Karen," he started, taking a step toward her, but Karen stepped away, shaking her head.

"No," she said, her voice cracking. There was a honk from outside, and she nodded to her kids. "We're leaving," she said, and Josh, Teddy, and Reid grabbed their things and headed for the door.

"I didn't—you weren't ever supposed to hear those things," my dad said, his voice getting more frantic. "I was just working. I was blowing off steam. I didn't mean anything—"

"I think maybe *I* didn't mean anything to you," Karen said. She was still crying, but I could hear a steely determination underneath her words now. "I mean, Paul, what were we think-ing, rushing into this?"

"What are you saying?" my dad asked, real fear in his voice now.

"I'm saying . . . I think we made a mistake," Karen said as the horn honked again, and she pulled the door open. "I just . . . need some time to think." She walked outside, slamming the door behind her, causing an awkward moment where Josh, Teddy, and Reid stared at the door, wondering if they were sup-posed to follow.

"Karen!" my dad yelled, sounding anguished as he yanked the door open and hurried outside behind her.

"Um . . ." Josh said, glancing at the door. "Think we should . . ." he started, but his voice trailed off, and there was an extremely uncomfortable pause, where nobody seemed to know where to look or what to say. After what felt like an eter-nity, my dad came back in, his shoulders hunched and his face ashen.

"Dad?" I asked tentatively, but he just shook his head and walked straight for his office, slamming the door behind him with enough force that I felt myself wince.

"Okay," Josh said, and then he, Reid, and Teddy were in motion, giving me waves and nods, all while hustling out the door like they couldn't get out of there fast enough.

Hallie walked more slowly toward the door, and I followed, feeling as shell-shocked as she looked.

"Well," she said. She bit her lip and looked in the direction of my dad's office, then turned to me, her expression troubled. I just nodded. I didn't know what else to say. What else *could* we say?

"I guess . . . I'll see you?" I said, trying to ignore the knot that had formed in my stomach. Hallie and I had done it—we'd done what we'd set out to do. We'd split our parents up. So why didn't it feel good at all? Why did it actually feel terrible?

"Yeah," Hallie said. She looked at me for a minute longer before giving me a nod and heading out the door. I closed the door behind her and leaned against it. I closed my eyes for just a moment, listening to the sound of the car drive away, not able to shake the feeling we'd just made a huge mistake.

CHAPTER 19

"Hello?" Sophie waved her hand in front of my face. "Gemma. Earth to Gemma. Come in, Gemma."

I looked across at her and smiled in the late-afternoon sunlight. I could tell it was probably getting close to five—the shadows were stretching long across the yard of Isabella and Olivia, the demon twins who Sophie had been babysitting for most of the summer. Right now the twins were running in circles all around our lounge chairs, and only occasionally hitting one of us with a water balloon. But I didn't mind, since it meant that Sophie and I had the whole afternoon together, since her idea of babysitting was very lax—she mostly left the kids to their own devices and only intervened if there was physical violence or if one of them needed medical attention. "Sorry," I said, making myself focus on my best friend, looking away from the shadows stretching over the grass. "What were you saying?"

Sophie sighed and gave me a knowing look. I glanced down at my hands. I was more than aware I had been out of it lately. Sophie had been beyond patient with me, but I had a feeling that patience might have just run out.

It had been two weeks since the day my dad and Karen had ended things. And while there hadn't been a drop of rain since, I hadn't quite been able to shake the feeling of walking around with a dark cloud over me. I didn't know how else to explain it—but I kept waiting to feel happy about what had happened, kept telling myself we had succeeded, that I *was* happy—only to find the happiness never came.

I had tried my best to shake it off, but it wasn't going easily. It was like when I'd forgotten to refill the generator tank—the same nagging feeling I'd left something undone, something unfinished. Except this time, there was no easy fix or solution.

"Sorry," I said, giving her an embarrassed grin, because I knew this was the umpteenth time I'd apologized to her. "What were you saying?"

She shot me an even look, one that let me know she wasn't going to be distracted quite as easily as that. "I was talking about Reid," she said. "About our date for tonight."

"Reid," I said, feeling myself smile at her for real. Sophie and Reid were absolutely smitten with each other, and I was thrilled to see it. Sophie had totally turned the corner from her bad-boy fixation, and I wasn't sure I'd ever seen Reid—or anyone, for that matter—quite so happy. He was practically levitating when he walked, and getting all the orders wrong at the ice-cream parlor. He'd told me the day before, with a huge smile on his face, that he was in danger of getting fired because of it, but he clearly couldn't care less. He was a man in love, and all the other consequences of this clearly meant nothing to him. "You know I think you two are totally cute together, right?"

"I know," Sophie said, and I could see she was blushing as she said it. I looked over her shoulder and saw a small demon child raising a water balloon in her direction, ready to strike.

"Incoming," I said, not even raising my voice that much. We'd been doing this all afternoon; by now we'd developed a system.

Sophie reached up and, without even looking, batted the water balloon away. It exploded on the grass, leaving both of us dry. "Awww." Isabella and Olivia sighed as they looked at it.

"Go do something else," I said, waving them off. "Something that doesn't involve bothering us." They both gave me a look that clearly indicated just how ridiculous that notion was, before they took off at a run, no doubt to find some new way to torture us.

"Enough about Reid," Sophie said in an incredibly unconvincing voice, and I laughed, since we both knew we'd be back to talking about Reid really quickly—probably within the next ten minutes. "Well, enough about Reid for now," she amended, shooting me a grin. "How's Ford?"

I felt myself smile, and it was like my heart was warmed up, like I'd just had a long drink of hot chocolate—that was the way I felt whenever I thought about him. He was the only thing that could cause the dark cloud to dissipate, in fact. "He's good," I said, unable to keep the goofy smile off my face, but not even really trying to. "We talked a little bit this morning. He's coming home next week."

Sophie raised her eyebrows at me. "How long, exactly?"

"Five days, eight hours, and nineteen minutes," I admitted as she laughed. "You know, approximately." Ford and I had been going strong ever since the night on the water. We'd only had about a week together before he'd had to go present his algorithm at the New Voices in Tech conference back in California. But we were talking and video-chatting constantly, and it was making the time pass—well, not quickly, but faster than it might have otherwise. It felt so natural to be with him, like it was something we should have been doing a long time ago. It wasn't like when I was with Teddy, and pretending to be someone I wasn't, because I was afraid he wouldn't like who I really was. And it wasn't like with Josh, when I'd *actually* been pretending to be someone I wasn't. Ford knew exactly who I was—he'd known me for my whole life, after all. He not only knew who I was and still liked me, he liked me *because* of who I was. And I knew him. After a summer of subterfuge and secrets and lies upon lies, it was such a relief to be with him—and to just be able to be myself.

Things were going so well, I wasn't even worried about what would happen in the fall, when he went back to school in California, and I went back to Connecticut. It just seemed like this was nothing more than a tiny roadblock—certainly, nothing we couldn't handle, if we were together.

"Gem, what's actually going on?" Sophie asked, and I felt my happy Ford-glow start to fade a little.

I looked over at my best friend and figured that the time had come to tell her—I couldn't keep half paying attention to every conversation we had for the remainder of the summer, after all. "It's my dad," I said. I didn't want to, but as I said it, a montage of what living with my dad for the last two weeks had been like flashed through my head. It had not been pretty. He'd taken this latest breakup harder than the first one—which made sense, because this time they'd actually gotten married. He was vacillating between working around the clock (to Bruce's delight) and lying on the couch at all hours, staring at the TV, not seeming even to care what was on. It was the reason I'd seen him watch three straight hours of the Home Shopping Network the other day, not once moving a muscle or calling in to buy anything, despite the low, low prices. He really wasn't handling it well—but he also wasn't reaching out to Karen, as far as I could tell. He seemed to think it was really over, once and for all.

"What about him?" Sophie asked, leaning closer to me.

"I . . . keep thinking maybe Hallie and I made a mistake. You know, splitting up him and Karen." I said this all in a rush, and it was something of a relief, even to say it out loud, like I'd just put down a heavy weight I'd been hauling around for far too long.

"Wow," Sophie said, raising her eyebrows. "I mean, I hate to say I told you so. . . ."

"What are you talking about?" I asked, shaking my head at her. "You love saying that. It's, like, your favorite thing to say."

"That's true," Sophie said, brightening. "Thanks so much for reminding me. I told you so."

"I should probably get used to hearing that," I said with a

grimace. "I think I'm going to be hearing pretty much the same thing from Ford."

"This is just proof you should never doubt us," Sophie said, and I laughed. "But seriously," she said, her expression growing more grave. "What are you going to do about it?"

"What do you mean?" I asked, blinking at her. Hallie and I had done what we'd set out to do. We'd broken them up. I felt bad about it, but done was done . . . wasn't it?

"I mean, if you really feel bad about this, you should fix it," she said, looking at me evenly. "If you can break them up, you can get them back together. Right?"

"Well . . ." I said. I didn't want to, but I kept flashing back to the morning after the storm, the look on Karen's face when she watched the footage making it clear this wasn't something she could just get over. "I'm not sure about that."

"You can at least *try*," Sophie said, her eyes still looking right into mine, not letting me off the hook for even a fraction of a second. "It's never too late for that. Right?"

I nodded. She *was* right. And the fact of the matter was, I didn't want this to be like the propane in the generator. I didn't want to be walking around with the feeling I'd done something wrong, or forgotten to do what I should have done. I wanted to take responsibility for once, and fix something and actually fix it right. And while I couldn't control what either my dad or Karen would do, I had to do my best to try to set right what I'd wrecked. And then, no matter what the outcome, I would not meddle in people's lives ever again. That I could be sure of.

"Right," I said. I pushed myself up to standing, then leaned down and gave Sophie a quick hug. "Thanks a lot."

"Oh, you know," Sophie said with false modesty. "It's what I'm here for." She raised an eyebrow at me. "So, where are you going to start?"

"Where I should have started first," I said, pulling out my phone and selecting one of my contacts. "I'm going to bring in some backup."

ᖆᖆᖆᖆᖆ

It was starting to get a little chilly by the time I made it to the beach. When I'd talked to Hallie on the phone, and I'd asked if she could meet and I'd mentioned today, I'd fully expected she'd say we should wait until tomorrow or the next day. But to my surprise, Hallie had wanted to meet today as soon as possible—which was my first indication she was feeling pretty much the same way I was about this situation.

Quonset beach was where Hallie and I had spent a lot of time together as kids, and so it just seemed right that we were meeting here again. Bruce's house was on the water, but I'd asked her to meet me by the front entrance instead. Not that I expected my dad to go wandering around, taking a midafternoon stroll down from the mansion, but you never knew, and I didn't want to have to spend our conversation looking over my shoulder, worrying someone might be overhearing what we were saying.

Hallie raised her hand to shield her eyes against the late-afternoon glare and then spotted me, waving from her place on the sand, halfway between the beach and the water. I waved back and, as I got closer, I suddenly realized I'd *missed* her. It was an emotion that caught me totally off guard. I'd been mad at Hallie and scared of her and irritated and challenged by her all summer—but missing her wasn't something I'd yet experienced. But there it was.

"Hey," I said, once I was in earshot. "How are you?"

"Good," she said immediately, then looked at me, and maybe saw some of what I was actually feeling on my face, and shook her head. "Not so good, actually," she said after a tiny pause. "I haven't actually been sleeping that well."

"Me neither," I said, giving her a sad smile. "Is it . . . about my dad and Karen?"

"Yes," Hallie said, her jaw falling in surprise as she looked at me. "It's bothering you, too?"

I nodded. "Every time I go to sleep, I just start seeing your mom's face when she saw the video," I said, and Hallie winced and nodded. "I keep thinking of what we should have done differently."

"Like, all of it," she said quietly, and I couldn't help but agree with her. What if we hadn't meddled at all? What if we'd spent the storm playing board games and bringing our parents breakfasts they might enjoy, as opposed to plotting against them and trying to give them allergy attacks?

"Yeah," I said. I glanced down at the time on my phone and nodded ahead of us. "Want to take a walk?" I asked. Hallie raised her eyebrows at me, and I shrugged. "I think better if I'm walking."

"Why not?" she said, and we started walking together, our footsteps in a line across the sand. "My mom's miserable," she said after we'd walked for a few moments in silence. "I've never seen her like this before. She's not eating, she's not writing. Mostly she just stays in bed. I'm worried about her. Josh is worried too."

"My dad's not doing great either," I admitted. Even though I was sorry Karen was going through this, I was actually happy to hear she was feeling just as bad as my dad was—it meant this might have an actual shot. If my dad was spending all day watching the Home Shopping Network, and Karen had moved on and was as happy as a clam, it would be a very different conversation. "So, what do we do about it?"

Hallie shot me a surprised look—I had a feeling it was similar to the one I'd given Sophie. "Do about it?"

"We caused this," I reminded her, and Hallie grimaced. "If we broke them up, we should be the ones to get them back together. We can at least try," I added, now knowing I was quoting Sophie almost word for word.

"You're right," Hallie said with a nod. I glanced down at my phone again and then stopped walking. She turned to face me. "So, what should we do?"

"Let's discuss that later tonight," I said, waving at the person who'd just walked onto the sand and was looking around, his brow furrowed. "Right now there's someone you need to talk to."

"What?" Hallie asked, turning to see what I was looking at and then growing pale when she saw it was Teddy who was walking toward us. "Gemma, what did you do?" she hissed as she frantically started smoothing down her hair with both hands.

"I decided I wasn't done trying to right wrongs," I said, motioning Teddy over more emphatically, because his steps had slowed significantly when he'd spotted Hallie and seemed to understand he'd been tricked.

"Gemma," he said as he walked up, sounding confused and not very happy with me at all. "You said Bruce wanted to meet with me about the movie he wants to base on my life."

"Yeah, that was a lie," I said with a shrug. "But he *is* currently talking to different nature filmmakers about doing a documentary on the peril of the marsh warbler."

Teddy's eyebrows flew up. "He *is*?"

"It may have been one of the ways Gwyneth is making things up to me," I said with a shrug. "She's got him convinced the youth market is really, really interested in birds."

"Wow," Teddy said, and he gave me a small smile. "That—that's great, Gemma. Thanks." His smile faded after a few seconds, though. "But that doesn't mean you should have lured me here under false pretenses—"

"Wait, I was lured here too," Hallie said, giving me a frown. "I didn't know you were going to be here," she said, glancing at Teddy before looking down at the sand again. "Gemma tricked both of us."

"Okay, both of you have now protested enough," I said, taking a step back so they were facing each other. "You both are unhappy without each other. So go be happy together."

They looked at each other for a long, silent moment, and then Teddy shook his head. "It's not that simple, Gemma."

"But what if it is?" I said as I looked between the two of

them—neither of them were looking away from the other, which was pretty much all the proof I needed that I'd done the right thing here. "Listen, I'm the last person who should want you two back together. And I do. So that should tell you something."

Hallie gave Teddy a small, tentative smile, and he took a tiny step closer to her. "Hey," Hallie said, her voice shaking with emotion.

"Hi," Teddy said back, his voice extra-deep, the way it got when he didn't want to let his feelings show too much.

"I miss you," Hallie said, her voice breaking.

"Me too," Teddy said, taking a step even closer to her—they were now just an inch or two apart, which was what I decided was my cue to leave. Just because I thought they were actually a good match and I wanted both of them to be happy, didn't mean I actually wanted to see the very extensive make-out session I had no doubt was coming any second.

"I'll see you guys," I said over my shoulder as I headed for the exit. Before I got there, though, I allowed myself one small glance back. And I saw Hallie and Teddy, not making out frantically like I'd been afraid of, but just wrapped in a hug, both of them holding the other so tight, it was like they weren't going to let go ever again. And, feeling like something had been set right, I felt myself smile as I walked to my car.

~~~~~~

I didn't really plan to go downtown, but I ended up driving that way, and when I saw there was an open parking space in front of Quonset Coffee, I swung into it immediately. It was getting close to dinnertime, but as far as I was concerned, that didn't also mean that it wasn't iced latte time.

The coffee shop was pretty deserted, and there was no line at the register as I ordered my usual iced latte. It wasn't until it had been made and I picked it up that I even noticed there was someone else in the coffee shop, someone I recognized—Josh.

I paused for a second and then crossed to his table, carrying my plastic cup. "Hey," I said, and he looked up and smiled at me.

"Hey," he said, nudging out the chair next to him with his foot. "Want to sit?"

"Sure," I said after only a moment's hesitation. I sat down and looked across the table at him. This was the new dynamic between us, but I found I liked it. We were friends, really friends, with no tension or anything charged between us. "So, what's going on?"

"Oh, you know," Josh said with a shrug. He gave me a tiny smile. "I've got a date tonight."

"Oh yeah?" I asked, leaning forward. Mostly, I was just relieved he was getting over Gwyneth, who'd gotten over him in record time and was now dating a guy she'd met at a Young Documentarians workshop. I wasn't sure, though, that Josh necessarily needed to know that.

"Yeah," he said, his smile widening. "I met her at the beach the other day. Her name's Madeline." He glanced over and shot me a look. "At least, she *says* her name's Madeline."

I couldn't help but laugh at that, and I leaned forward, listening, as Josh started to tell me the story.

CHAPTER 20

"I don't know why we're doing this," my dad grumbled from where he was slumped against the window of Bruce's SUV.

"Because I thought an afternoon hike would be fun," I said, trying to make my voice bright and cheerful and not at all suspicious, or reveal what I was really feeling at the moment—totally stressed-out. "Doesn't that sound fun?" I peered at the screen on my phone, which was on the map feature and telling me I was currently going the wrong way, as texts from Hallie flashed fast and furiously across the screen.

Hallie Bridges
Where are you?

Hallie Bridges
Why aren't you here yet? I can only stall for so long!

Hallie Bridges

She wants to leave. She's trying to get me to go, and I'm not going to be able to keep her here much longer.

Hallie Bridges

SERIOUSLY, WHERE ARE YOU?

Since I knew I couldn't text while I was driving—or ask my dad to text for me, if I wanted to have a shot of any of this being a secret—all Hallie's texts were doing was managing to raise my stress level even more, and it had been pretty high to begin with, considering what we were going to try to pull off.

"Sure," my dad said with a long sigh as he looked out the window again. It had taken almost a full hour of cajoling to get him off the couch and to agree to come with me. For a moment there it looked like he was going to refuse to do it, which had sent me into a panic, since I couldn't exactly tell him *why* I needed him to just agree to come with me—I couldn't tell him his potential future happiness might depend on it, or anything like that.

Apparently, Karen had been much easier to convince, because Hallie seemed to have no sympathy for what was happening on my end. I just hoped my dad's reluctance to get out the door—coupled with my wrong turns—weren't enough to put this whole thing in danger.

I glanced down at my phone again, feeling the sweat start to form on my temples, and saw that, somehow, I'd found my way onto the right road again. I could feel the relief start coursing through my body as I saw I was only a few minutes away. Which meant I would have just enough time to say what I needed to say.

"Dad," I said, with enough emphasis that my father raised his head from the window and blinked at me.

"What?" he asked, sounding confused by my tone. "Is everything okay? Do we have to turn around or something?" He really wasn't able to hide the hope in his voice that the answer to the last question would be yes.

"No," I said firmly. "We're not turning around. I needed to talk to you about something."

"Okay," he said, his voice wary. I wasn't sure the wariness was just because of his current depressed state, either. The fact was, my dad and I weren't great at talking about our feelings— or anything, really, that went beyond the easy, light conversations we tended to stick with. But just because that had been the case, didn't mean it had to continue that way. After all, I'd tried surfing. There was no saying what could be accomplished.

"So here's the thing," I said as I glanced down at my GPS and then turned down a road that seemed more dirt than pavement. I parked next to the Jeep I recognized as Hallie's, and was just hoping my dad was too distracted to recognize it as well. We both got out of the car, and he looked at me across the hood of the SUV as he did some halfhearted hamstring stretches.

"What's the thing?" he asked, his brow furrowed.

I nodded toward the direction we would be going, and either my dad had never been there before, or he wasn't paying attention, but either way, he didn't say anything about the fact that we were headed for Pearson's Bluff. "I never should have gone behind your back and tried to mess up your personal life," I said. "And I'm really, really sorry for any trouble I caused you."

My dad's steps slowed, and he turned to face me. "Thank you, Gemma," he said after a moment. "That's . . . I appreciate you saying that."

"But here's the thing," I said, starting to walk again, my dad falling into step next to me. "I acted the way I did because I was blindsided. If you'd told me, back when I was a kid, that you were dating Karen, I might have handled it better." My dad blinked at me in surprise, like this was the first time he'd ever put this together. "And," I went on, knowing I had to get this out before I lost my nerve, "you should have told me you were dating her again this summer. You can't just tell your daughter you're *married* to someone out of the blue."

My dad nodded, and we walked in silence for a moment before he looked over at me. "I hear what you're saying," he said, finding his words slowly, like he was thinking about each one before he spoke. "I guess . . . I'm not the best when it comes to this stuff."

"I'm not either," I admitted, giving him a half-smile. "But maybe we can get better at it together?"

"We can certainly try," my dad said, reaching over and giving my hair a pat, the same way he used to when I was little. Normally I hated this, but right now I found I didn't really mind it so much, somehow. "Well, we can at least try next time," he said after a moment of silence, the sadness in his voice returning at full force. "If there is a next time."

"What about Karen?" I asked, slowing my steps slightly—if possible, I wanted to time it just right.

My dad shook his head. "I think that's over," he said, and I could hear it in his voice—how much he wished this wasn't the case. "She said she's never going to see me again."

I nodded ahead of us, feeling myself smile. "You sure about that?"

My dad looked up, and his jaw dropped. There, standing by the edge of the bluff, were Karen and Hallie. Hallie was shooting me looks that were very clearly saying *What took you so long?* But I don't think either of our parents noticed—they were just looking right at each other.

"Gemma," my dad said, even though he hadn't taken his eyes from Karen. "What are you doing?"

"Righting a wrong," I said, going over to stand next to Hallie.

"We both are," she added.

Karen looked away from my dad, and between me and her daughter. "The two of you . . . working together?" she asked. "What is he even doing here?" she asked Hallie, crossing her arms.

"You said it was your favorite place in the world," Hallie said with a shrug.

"The most romantic place ever," I added as Karen's jaw dropped open.

"How did you two know that?" she asked faintly.

"We just thought there was something you should see," Hallie said as she reached into the purse between her feet and pulled out her iPad.

"I don't think I want to see anything else," my dad said, and Karen took a small step away.

"I agree with Paul," she said, her voice low and hurt. "I think I've seen enough."

Hallie and I exchanged a glance. This was what we'd pretty much spent the last week doing. If they didn't see it, I wasn't sure how much of a chance we'd have to fix it. "It'll just take a minute," I said, hoping they couldn't hear the desperation in my tone. "What's the harm?"

Hallie held out her tablet, apparently not waiting for an answer, and started to play the video. And maybe it was against their better judgment, but both of our parents took a step closer as the video started to play.

It was the opposite of the first video we'd made—and it had been a lot easier to find the footage. It was every shot of my dad being smitten and in love with Karen. Every clip of him telling her how happy she made him, every shot of her smiling at him, utterly in love. Like we'd hoped, they both took a step closer as they looked at the video playing, and Hallie handed off her iPad without either of them noticing. Hallie and I took another step away as they took a step closer together, both of them looking at she screen as the truth of what they had played out for them.

When the video ended, there were tears in Karen's eyes, and my dad seemed to be clearing his throat a lot more than he normally did. "I'm so sorry, my love," my dad said, and Karen looked up at him.

"Me too," she whispered, but before I could see what happened next, Hallie stuck her hand in front of my eyes.

"What was that?" I asked her, trying to get visibility back.

"Old people kissing," she said, and I could hear the shudder in her voice. "I did it for your own good."

I nodded, thankful to be spared this. "Thanks," I said as I turned away, and Hallie walked a few steps apart, letting our parents have their privacy. But the very fact that they *needed* to have their privacy was a good thing. A really good thing. It meant we'd pulled this off.

"So what now?" Hallie asked me as we stopped walking and she turned to me.

I blinked at her, realizing I didn't know. We'd been so focused on reversing our Reverse Parent Trap—which Hallie had spent the last week telling me could just be called a regular Parent Trap, even though I'd preferred the sound of the other one—we hadn't focused much on what came next. But whatever it was, I somehow wasn't worried. Hallie and I had both spent so much time and energy trying to destroy each other, now that we were on the same side, I had a feeling that whatever came next, we'd be able to handle it. "I don't know," I finally said with a smile, realizing she was still waiting for an answer. "But I guess we'll figure it out."

"Girls?" I looked over and saw that Karen was gesturing for us. My dad's arm was around her shoulders, and her head was resting against his chest. If the old-person make-out session hadn't done it, this was the proof we needed—they were now back together again.

"What do you think?" Hallie asked, tipping her head toward our parents. "Should we go?"

I looked over at them and then back at Hallie. I knew this was the end of one chapter. That after this, everything was going to change. I let out a long breath and then nodded. "Let's do it," I said.

Hallie gave me a smile, and we fell into step together as we walked over to join our parents.

EPILOGUE

I looked out at the water, feeling my dress blow around my ankles. It had been a perfect end-of-summer day, clear and not too hot. Which meant it was perfect for what was about to happen.

I heard someone call my name, and I turned to see Gemma running toward me. Before I could reply, though, she had reached me, one hand holding her hair back from her face.

"Oh my gosh, Hallie," she said, talking a mile a minute. "Where have you been? They want to get started, and you know we're the first ones down the aisle. Rosie is *freaking out*. Don't let me get back on her bad side. She's barely forgiven me for letting the generator die during the storm."

"Sorry," I said, instinctively looking around. Even though this wasn't a real wedding—it was hard to have one of those when the couple had already gotten married beforehand—it was decided pretty quickly that this was what was needed, and it was the perfect way to close out the summer properly. Basically just a reaffirming of my mom and Paul's vows, but with a big party afterward—and in front of all the family and friends who hadn't been included—or told about it—the first time around.

It became clear early on that the only place my mom wanted to have it was at Pearson's Bluff, the place where she and Paul had realized how much they wanted to be together—thanks in no small part to Gemma and me. Whenever either one of us tried to take credit for getting them back together, though, we were usually reminded that we were the ones who'd split them up in the first place, so we'd pretty much stopped mentioning it—at least not while they were within earshot. Since we had basically two weeks to pull off a wedding, we'd turned to Rosie, who'd jumped into action. She'd pulled everything off beautifully, and Bruce had footed the bill for everything; he'd just made my mom and Paul sign away their life rights as a condition. He was already having writers working on their story, convinced that their story of love, lost and found and lost (and found) again, would make for a great opening weekend. "Is everything ready?"

"Everything but us," she said as she reached out and straightened a piece of my hair. She nodded down at the dress I was wearing. "Nice outfit."

I felt myself laugh as I looked at hers, which was identical to mine—long, light-pink chiffon that blew with the slightest hint of a wind. If someone had told me even a few weeks ago that I would be wearing matching dresses with Gemma, I wouldn't have believed it for anything. I was happy to be doing it now, though. Happier than I could even put into words.

"Girls!" I looked over and saw Rosie rushing up to us, barking orders into her earpiece as she went. "Hallie, where have you been?"

"Sorry," I said immediately. I hadn't known Rosie that long, but she'd had this effect on me right away. "I just needed a moment."

"Well, I hope you took it, because we're running three behind."

"Ready," I said, giving her a nod.

"Okay," she said into her headset. Then she gave Gemma a quick hug and shot me a smile. "Let's take this through to the ending we rehearsed," she said, giving Gemma a nudge toward the makeshift aisle that had been set up and which led to the end of the bluff.

As I looked down it, I could see why Rosie had been so fixated on the time—a gorgeous sunset was just about to start.

"Here we go," Gemma said, shooting me a smile as I took my place next to her. From the side, I could hear the string quartet start playing, and we began walking together, keeping pace the way we'd practiced at the rehearsal dinner.

I let myself look from side to side as I walked—I couldn't help it. Josh was already standing up at the front with the other groomsman—Bruce, who was already sobbing into a mono-grammed handkerchief. Apparently, weddings made him weepy. Gwyneth had appointed herself the videographer, de-spite the fact that nobody had actually asked her to do this, and she was crouched by the front row, camera glued to her eye. Sophie and Reid were sitting together, Sophie grinning at both of us, Reid smiling only at her.

I passed Teddy as I walked, and I gave him a tiny wave, and he winked at me. Things had been really good with us so far. We were taking it slow—sometimes it felt like we were totally starting over, both of us being honest about everything this time around. But it was good. It felt like the beginning of something real.

I saw Gemma was smiling at Ford, who was sitting at the edge of the front row, dressed up in a suit and tie. Ford had the same besotted look in his eyes he'd had ever since they'd gotten together. They were beyond happy together, and though the four of us hadn't exactly gotten around to doing things like going on double dates, I figured that, at some point, we just might.

Gemma and I reached the end of the aisle and took our places off to the side. She shot me a look I was able to read right away—excitement mixed with nervousness mixed with happiness. I knew exactly what she meant, since I was feeling pretty much the same way.

I gave my sister a smile and then let out a breath. I turned to look down the aisle, ready for what came next.

And as the musicians went into the wedding march, and everyone stood up, I realized Rosie had actually been wrong. This wasn't an ending after all.

It was actually a beginning.

ACKNOWLEDGMENTS

First and foremost, I must thank my brilliant editor, Anna Roberto. Thank you for believing in these books from the beginning, and always seeing the perfect way to make them better. It's been such a fun journey to take with you!

Thank you to Jean Feiwel and all the wonderful people at Macmillan. I'm beyond lucky to be part of such an amazing team! Thank you to Liz Szabla, Caitlin Sweeny, Nicole Banholzer, Allison Verost, Molly Brouillette, Mary Van Aiken, Lauren Burniac, Kathryn Little, Ashley Halsey, and Kaitlin Severini.

Thank you to Rich Deas for these amazing covers!

Thank you to my wonderful agent, Emily Van Beek, who heard this idea first and wanted to know more.

Thank you to Jessi for the beach retreats and Jessica for the mountain retreats. You guys are the best.

And finally, thanks and love to my family—Mom, Jason, Katie, and Murphy.

READ THE WHOLE
BROKEN HEARTS AND REVENGE
TRILOGY.

"I love this series! Katie Finn is an author to watch!"
—Morgan Matson, bestselling author of THE UNEXPECTED EVERYTHING, on the Broken Hearts and Revenge Trilogy

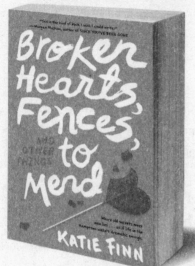

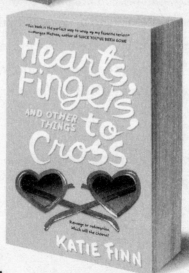